"No woman will ever be loved as I am going to love you."

He carried her to the bed and laid her down on it, his expression saying all that needed to be said as he looked at her for a long moment.

Anna took hold of his hand and placed it on her stomach, pressing it gently into the swollen hardness. "Love me, Ben," she whispered. "Please."

It was all the invitation he required.

Anna closed her eyes as passion claimed her, letting her heart have its way and her head be silenced. Maybe this was wrong and she would regret it, but she couldn't bear to stop what was happening. She couldn't bear to deny herself this time in Ben's arms even if it was a mistake!

1.85

Dear Reader,

The Baby Issue focuses on a topic that arouses strong emotions in a lot of people: surrogacy.

As I researched the background for this story, I was in contact with several women who had been childless until a member of their immediate families had offered to be a surrogate for them. Their tales were inspirational, and I am indebted to them for sharing their experiences with me.

I hope that you will read this book with an open mind and heart, and feel as I did that my heroine, Anna, made the right decision when she offered to have a baby for her sister. It seemed only right that she should find the perfect man in Ben Cole to share her life with after all the heartache she had been through. There is nothing better than a happy ending!

My very best wishes to you all,

Jennifer Taylor

The
Baby Issue

Jennifer Taylor

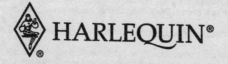

HARLEQUIN®

TORONTO • NEW YORK • LONDON
AMSTERDAM • PARIS • SYDNEY • HAMBURG
STOCKHOLM • ATHENS • TOKYO • MILAN • MADRID
PRAGUE • WARSAW • BUDAPEST • AUCKLAND

ISBN 0-373-06342-3

THE BABY ISSUE

First North American Publication 2001

CHAPTER ONE

THE taxi had dropped her off outside the surgery. Anna Clemence took a deep breath as it drove away.

She was on her own now.

She had made her decision and there was no going back on it. She owed it to Jo to do the very best she could.

A shadow darkened her grey eyes as she thought about her sister. It was a month since Jo had died yet she still found it hard to believe that she would never see her again. Jo had always been there for her in the past but now she had to stand on her own two feet. There would be no one to turn to in the coming months, no one to offer emotional or financial support. She only had herself to rely on from now on.

Anna picked up her suitcase then pushed open the surgery door. Dr Adam Knight, the senior partner at the practice, had explained that he couldn't be there to meet her that morning. However, he had assured her that his colleague, Benedict Cole, was expecting her. Now, as she joined the queue in front of the reception desk, Anna couldn't help hoping that she wouldn't have to wait long to see Dr Cole. She had been up since five that morning and she was starting to flag.

'I'm Anna Clemence,' she began when she reached the desk. However, the middle-aged receptionist didn't give her time to finish.

'Oh, you must be the new practice nurse! Ben said that you would be arriving this morning. I'll just give him a buzz to let him know that you're here.'

The woman quickly relayed the message then smiled at her. 'Ben said to tell you that he'll be free in a few minutes, so why don't you take your case through to the staffroom and wait in there? It's been like a madhouse in here this morning. It's supposed to be emergencies only on Saturdays so I don't know where they've all come from!'

'Thanks.' Anna smiled back, warmed by the older woman's friendly manner. 'I'll do that.'

She made her way through the door at the rear of the waiting room and quickly found the staffroom. Putting down her case, she went to the window and looked out but there wasn't much to see apart from the car park.

She turned and looked around the room instead, smiling when she saw the mismatched assortment of crockery stacked on the draining board and the extra-large jar of coffee strategically placed next to the kettle. The room was almost a replica of any number of staffrooms at places where she had worked in the past so that she felt instantly at home. Was it a good omen? She hoped so. She needed all the luck she could get at the moment.

'Hi, there. Sorry you've had to wait. I don't know what's come over everyone today. Saturdays are *never* usually this busy!'

Anna looked round as a man appeared. The room was rather dark so that she couldn't see him clearly at first. She just had an impression of someone tall with fair hair before he switched on the light.

He had to be at least six feet tall, she decided, taking rapid stock as he came towards her, with a leanly muscular physique which the conservative navy trousers and paler blue shirt he was wearing couldn't disguise. His hair was a rich sandy-blond colour rather than merely fair, the kind of shade that a woman would pay a small fortune for at the hairdresser's, she thought inconsequentially.

With hair that colour she expected his eyes to be blue, so it came as a surprise to see that they were a very dark brown, the same colour as his eyebrows. It was only when she noticed the amusement they held that she realised she had been staring at him and quickly looked away.

'I'm Ben Cole,' he said, offering her his hand. 'Adam explained that he couldn't be here to meet you, I believe?'

'He did.' Anna fixed a smile to her mouth as she shook hands, hoping that her discomfort didn't show. Ben Cole was a very attractive man and it probably wasn't the first time he'd caught a woman staring at him. However, it wouldn't do to give him the wrong impression. 'He said that you'd let me have the keys to the flat.'

'I've got them right here.' He handed her a bunch of keys then looked round, frowning when he spotted her suitcase by the door. 'Is that all you've brought with you?'

'I didn't think I needed anything else,' she replied quickly, deeming it wiser not to explain that the case held all her worldly goods. It would only give rise to more questions and that was something she wanted to avoid at all costs.

She experienced a momentary qualm as she wondered what would happen when Ben Cole and his colleagues found out what she had omitted to tell them. *Legally* she'd had no need to say anything, of course. There were rules governing the type of questions that could be asked at an interview, so she hadn't done anything wrong by withholding the information, though she knew that it would have been common courtesy to have mentioned the fact before she had accepted the post. Now all she could hope was that by the time she was forced to tell everyone the truth, she would have proved herself capable of doing the job.

'Probably not.' Ben treated her to an openly quizzical look. 'I don't suppose it was worth bringing too much stuff with you when you're only going to be here for four months or so. To be honest, I was surprised when Adam told me that he had found someone willing to take the job. Not many people are interested in short-term contracts, especially not someone with your experience. I believe you used to work at St Luke's in London. In the renal unit, wasn't it?'

'That's right,' Anna replied, feeling her nervousness increase when she heard the curiosity in his voice. 'I dealt mainly with children and teenagers, doing home support visits to those who were undergoing dialysis or were hoping to have a kidney transplant. I really enjoyed it, too.'

'So what made you decide to give it up?' he asked with a heavy frown. 'It seems a strange thing to do, especially if you enjoyed the work so much. Taking this post doesn't strike me as a career move.'

Anna bit back a groan as she realised that she only had herself to blame for giving him an opening to ask more questions. She really must be more careful and watch what she said.

'I had to move back to Cheshire to be nearer to my sister. She…well, she needed me here and I moved in with her for a while,' she finished lamely, wishing she had never got into this conversation in the first place.

'Really? Why was that?' Ben leant against the sink unit and studied her thoughtfully. Anna could feel his warm brown eyes travelling over her face and had a sudden mental image of the reflection she had seen in the mirror that morning. She sighed.

The past weeks had taken their toll and there was no escaping the fact that she looked vastly different to how she had previously. She wasn't vain but she knew that a lot of men had found the combination of lustrous black hair and a porcelain-fine complexion attractive in the past.

She'd always thought that her mouth was too big but several had remarked that it was her best feature. Others had commented on her deep grey eyes, framed by lashes so thick and black she never needed to use mascara. However, that had been then and the reflection she had seen that morning had born little resemblance to how she had looked once upon a time.

'My sister had endometrial cancer. Unfortunately, they didn't find out what was wrong with her until it was fairly advanced,' she explained, realising that he was waiting for her to answer his question. She shrugged but she could feel the pain biting deep inside her once again. 'The doctors did all they could, and at one point we thought that Jo was going to make it, but it turned out that there were second-aries. She d-died a month ago.'

Anna swallowed hard because she didn't want to make a fool of herself by breaking down in front of him. She jumped when he suddenly reached out and squeezed her hand.

'I'm sorry. I know how hard it is to deal with something like that, especially in our line of work. You tend to think that you should be able to find a cure for everything, but sadly that isn't the case.'

Anna looked up when she heard the pain in his voice. 'Did you lose someone close to you through illness?'

'Yes. That's why I know what you must be going through.' He gave her hand a final squeeze then let it go. 'Anyway, let's get you up to the flat and then I'd better get back to work before Eileen has a riot on her hands!'

She laughed softly because she knew that he was making a deliberate effort to lighten the mood. It was obvious that whatever had happened in Ben's past still hurt him and she couldn't help wondering what had gone on before it struck her that it was none of her business. She, more than anyone, should understand his desire not to talk about it.

He picked up her case and led the way to a staircase at the end of the hall. 'There's another flight of steps leading up to the flat from the car park, so you can come and go that way rather than having to trail through the surgery. However, it's handy being able to use these stairs of a morning. I know Beth found it useful.'

'Beth's the nurse who I'm covering for, isn't she?' Anna asked, following him upstairs.

'That's right.' He glanced over his shoulder as they reached the top of the stairs. 'She used to live in the flat before she moved in with Adam.'

'You mean Dr Knight?' she asked, frowning.

'That's right.' He laughed as he put her case down by the door. 'It's a long story which I really don't have time to go into at the moment. But if you ever get the chance, ask Beth to tell you all about it. I never used to believe in fate but I do now!'

Anna laughed. 'That sounds very intriguing.'

'Oh, it is, believe me!' He smiled at her and she felt a trickle of heat flow through her veins when she saw the warmth in his eyes. 'Anyhow, I'd love to stay and talk to you for longer but I really must go. We're usually finished by eleven so if there's anything you need, just give me a shout.'

'Thank you,' she said softly. Maybe it was silly but she couldn't help noticing that he was looking at her like a man looked at a woman he found attractive.

'Oh, and in case I forgot to say it before, I'll say it now— welcome to Winton surgery, Anna. I hope you'll be very happy here, even if it *is* only for a short time.'

He disappeared down the stairs before she could reply. Anna heard him speaking to someone at the bottom, heard a burst of laughter flow up the stairs and smiled. Maybe it was a bit too soon to make up her mind but she had a feeling that she was going to be very happy here. She sensed that she could grow to like Ben Cole once she got to know him better and...

And what? a small voice whispered in her mind. What if she did grow to like him? What if he liked her? What if they found each other attractive, even? Exactly what did she hope would come out of it? What future could there be for a woman in her situation?

Anna felt the little bubble of happiness burst. Her future was all mapped out and there was no place in it for Benedict Cole or any other man!

Anna spent the next hour unpacking and finding out where everything was kept. Although the flat was small there was everything there that she would need, which was a good job, bearing in mind how little she had brought with her.

She had lived in staff accommodation in her last job so she'd not had to worry about furniture and crockery or the hundred and one other things needed to set up a home. It hadn't been a priority when she had moved in with Jo either, but at some point soon she would have to make provision to buy all those things, even though she had no idea where she would get the money from. After all, there wasn't just herself to think about now.

She sighed as she felt a familiar wave of panic wash over her. She had promised herself that she would try to remain positive but it wasn't easy when she knew the difficulties she was going to face. All she could do was keep reminding herself that she wasn't the first woman to have found herself in this situation, even if the circumstances were rather unusual in her case. Other people had managed and so would she!

That decided, she went into the kitchen to make herself a cup of tea. It was only when she opened the fridge that she realised she didn't have any milk or tea bags—or anything else for that matter. In the rush to get packed that morning to leave her sister's home, she had given no thought to the subject of groceries, but she would have to do something about it soon.

She fetched her bag then went to the back door, hunting through the bunch of keys Ben Cole had given her to find the one that fitted the lock. She tried several in turn but none of them worked. It left her with no choice but to use the exit through the surgery, even though she had wanted to avoid doing that until she was officially on duty.

Anna started down the stairs then paused when she heard a commotion break out below. She could hear a woman screaming but she couldn't make out what she was saying. She hurried down the rest of the stairs and followed the noise to the waiting room, taking in the scene that met her at a glance.

'Give him to me,' she ordered, rushing forward and taking the child from the terrified mother's arms. It was a little boy, about two years old, and he was deeply unconscious, his eyes rolled back into his head and his lips tinged blue. Putting her ear to the child's chest, Anna assured herself that he was still breathing then turned to Eileen.

'Which way is the treatment room?'

'This way. I'll show you.'

Eileen flew out from behind the desk and led the way, opening the door to the treatment room for her. The child's mother was sobbing hysterically now so that Anna had to raise her voice to be heard.

'Tell Dr Cole that we need him in here straight away, please.'

Anna didn't waste any time as the receptionist hurried

away. She laid the little boy on the couch and quickly un-zipped his coat. 'When did this happen?' she asked the sobbing mother.

'Just a few moments ago. Sam was up most of the night with earache, which is why I brought him to the surgery this morning.' The young woman wiped her eyes with the back of her hand. 'He felt really hot when I dressed him and he wouldn't eat his breakfast, which just isn't like him. He seemed all right when we got here but then he went all…all stiff and started twitching.'

'I see.' Anna slipped off the child's coat and quickly removed his jumper and trousers as well. Hurrying to the sink, she filled a bowl with tepid water then looked round when Ben Cole appeared.

'What have we got?' he asked, hurrying to the couch.

'He appears to have had a convulsion. His temperature is elevated so I was about to sponge him down,' she reported crisply, carrying the bowl back to the couch. 'His mother says that he was complaining of earache through the night.'

'Fine. You get on with that while I check him over.' He didn't say anything more as he quickly set about examining the little boy, but Anna had seen the approval in his brown eyes and she felt her heart lift.

It was nice to know that Ben appreciated her efforts, she thought as she started sponging the child's hot skin. Maybe it was silly to set any store by his opinion but she knew that it meant a lot to her.

'Classic signs of a febrile convulsion,' he said, *sotto voce*, glancing at her. 'See how flushed his face and neck are, and the rigidity of the limbs and slight arching of the spine.'

'I thought it was that,' she said, equally softly. She ran

the damp cloth over the little boy's chest once again. 'I think this is helping, though.'

'It is. The best thing you can do in a case like this is to cool the child down.' He grimaced. 'Sorry. I don't need to tell you that, obviously!'

Anna laughed at his rueful expression. 'Don't worry. You can't afford to be thin-skinned when you're a nurse. Most doctors seem to believe that they are the fount of all knowledge.'

'Ouch! I'll have to watch my step in future, Nurse Clemence. I wouldn't want to trip over my ego in front of you and end up flat on my face.'

His eyes were teasing, making it clear that he knew that she'd been joking. Anna smiled back before she realised how dangerous it was to let the conversation continue in that vein. She had to remember that this job was simply a stopgap and not get involved with the people she worked with. It would make it that less painful when the time came for her to leave.

She carried on sponging the little boy and was rewarded when he started to come round a few minutes later. Ben turned to the child's mother and smiled reassuringly at her.

'He's back with us again. I know it's been a shock for you but try not to let him see that you're upset. We want to keep him as calm as possible to give him time to recover.'

'He will be all right, won't he?' the girl asked shakily, digging a crumpled tissue out of her pocket and scrubbing her eyes with it.

Anna took the bowl of water to the sink and emptied it away then plucked a handful of clean tissues from the box on the counter and gave them to her. She hadn't realised how young the mother was until that moment because she'd been too busy dealing with the child to pay much attention to her. Now she couldn't help sighing when she realised that the girl was little more than a child herself.

'He should be fine. He's had what we call a febrile convulsion, which isn't nearly as scary as it sounds.' Ben drew the girl forward then gently picked up the little boy and placed him in her arms. 'All it means is that the bit of his brain that usually lowers the temperature when it gets too high didn't work properly. I believe you said that he had earache last night?'

He carried on when she nodded. 'He probably has an ear infection and that's what caused his temperature to rise. I'll check him over once he's recovered properly but I don't want you to worry too much. A lot of small children have febrile convulsions but they usually grow out of them.'

'Does that mean it could happen again?' the girl asked worriedly, hugging the whimpering child to her.

'It's possible, but you can do a lot to prevent it happening again by taking some simple precautions like giving him paracetamol at the first signs of fever and sponging him down,' he explained calmly.

'I wish I'd known that,' she said miserably. 'If I'd realised I could give him paracetamol I would have done so.'

'You must make sure that it's one formulated for young children,' he warned her. 'And that you don't exceed the dosage. However, there are a number of very good products you can buy over the counter.'

'Do they cost a lot?' The girl shrugged but Anna could see the flush that had risen to her cheeks. 'I'm on my own, you see, and some of these things cost a lot of money...'

She tailed off, not that she needed to say anything else. Anna turned away because she was afraid of what might be written on her face at that moment. She ran water into the sink and washed the bowl, barely listening as Ben explained that he would include a child-safe analgesic on the prescription so that Sam's mother wouldn't need to buy it.

'Anna.'

She jumped when Ben touched her arm, feeling the colour rushing to her face when she saw the concern in his eyes.

'Are you all right?' he asked softly.

'Fine. I was just trying to catch my breath,' she explained hurriedly.

'No wonder. It's been a real baptism of fire and you're not even officially on duty yet,' he agreed, but she could tell that he hadn't fully believed her explanation.

Fortunately, little Sam started crying in earnest at that point so he had no time to question her further. Anna realised that she had to be more careful in future and make sure that she separated her personal feelings from her professional responsibilities. She couldn't afford to let one affect the other if she hoped to get through the coming months.

Ben quickly examined the little boy and, as suspected, it turned out that Sam had an ear infection. Anna stayed with them because she didn't think it was right to leave even though the crisis was over. The little boy was obviously very distressed and his mother, who had told them that her name was Lucy Wilkins, didn't look much better.

Ben drew Anna aside while the young mother tried to console the screaming toddler. 'I know this is a huge imposition, but would you mind if I left Sam and Lucy with you while I finish seeing the rest of my patients? I want to make sure that he's all right before she takes him home.'

'Of course I don't mind,' Anna assured him. She glanced at the sobbing child and sighed. 'He's really upset, poor little mite.'

'He must be in a lot of pain because the infection is quite

severe, especially in his left ear. I've got some sample sachets of analgesic in my room so maybe you could get some of that down him.'

He grimaced as the little boy started screaming louder than ever. 'You might have more luck than his mum. I get the impression that she's been having a rough time with him of late, not that it's any surprise. It isn't easy, bringing up a child on your own.'

'It isn't,' Anna agreed hollowly. She summoned a smile when Ben looked at her, afraid that he would tell that the comment had touched a nerve. 'If you let me have that analgesic, I'll see if Sam will take it from me.'

'Thanks, Anna. I really appreciate this.'

Ben hurried back to his room and came back a few minutes later with a sachet of the analgesic, but he didn't stop. Anna knew that he must be anxious to get back to his other patients so she merely took it from him then set about finding a plastic measuring spoon in one of the drawers. Little Sam was sobbing his heart out by that time, his face bright red with temper and pain, and Lucy had tears in her eyes as well.

'I don't know what to do when he gets like this,' she admitted helplessly. 'Sometimes he screams so hard that he makes himself sick and I don't know how to stop him.'

'It isn't easy, dealing with a toddler,' Anna consoled her. 'A lot of parents have trouble coping.'

'It must be easier if there are two of you, though,' Lucy said, struggling to hold onto Sam as he arched his back in an attempt to free himself. 'I keep worrying in case I'm doing everything wrong. It would be lovely to have someone to share all the problems,' she added wistfully.

Anna bit back a sigh because she understood exactly how the girl felt. 'I'm sure that it must be difficult at times but you're doing a great job. Sam is obviously loved and that's the most important thing. Now, do you think it would help if I took him for a moment? If we can calm him down we can give him some of this analgesic.'

Lucy gratefully relinquished the screaming toddler into her care. Anna took firm hold of the squirming little body and stood up. 'Now, Sam, I know that you don't feel well but you'll feel a lot better if you stop crying.'

The child stared at her with huge, tear-soaked eyes, obviously shocked at being parted so summarily from his mother. Anna smiled reassuringly at him. 'Shall we see what we can find to play with? I don't know if there are any toys in these cupboards but we can have a look.'

She set him down on the floor and started opening the cupboards. 'Oh, look what I've found!'

She hauled out a big plastic tub of building blocks and tipped them onto the carpet. Sam immediately crouched down, his tears momentarily forgotten as he picked up two of the blocks and tried to fit them together.

'Like this. See?' Anna showed him how to slot the blocks together, smiling when he immediately copied her. She glanced over her shoulder as he picked up two more. 'He's very bright, isn't he? I only needed to show him once and he knew what to do.'

Lucy smiled. 'He does seem to be quick on the uptake,' she agreed proudly. 'I bought a big box of toys from the charity shop in town and it was amazing how quickly he learned how to use them. And he just loves it when I read to him. He knows some of the stories off by heart now.'

'Story?' Sam said hopefully, looking up.

Anna laughed as she ruffled his blond curls. 'Later, poppet. I'm sure Mummy will read to you when you get home.'

He gave her a beaming smile then went back to his building work. He seemed quite content so she decided that it might be a good moment to see if he would take the analgesic. She snipped the top off the sachet then measured out the recommended dosage and crouched beside him.

'Are you going to be a good boy and take this for me, Sam?' she asked, offering him the spoon.

He stared at the bright pink liquid for a moment then obediently opened his mouth. Anna smiled as he swallowed the whole spoonful without a murmur.

'That's a good boy. Well done!' she exclaimed, giving him a hug.

'I hope he takes it from me as easily,' Lucy said worriedly. 'And Dr Cole said that he's going to need ear drops as well. I don't know if I'll be able to make him sit still long enough to get them in his ears.'

'Do it while you're reading to him,' Anna advised her. 'I used to work with children and I always found that it was best to choose a quiet moment if you wanted to give them any medication. But if he does get upset, don't make a big issue out of it. Just wait until he calms down then have another go.'

'I'll do that.' Lucy sighed. 'I wish there was someone to ask about things like that. I do my best but there are all sorts of things that crop up and I'm not sure how to deal with them.'

'Don't you have any family?' Anna asked, handing a bright green block to the little boy.

'No. I was brought up in care. There's just Sam and me, but we muddle through as best we can.'

'Well, you seem to be doing a fine job to me. Sam is a lovely little boy.' Anna smiled at the girl but she couldn't deny that her heart had started aching when she'd heard that. It had struck a bit too close to home. It was a relief when Ben appeared and informed them that he had finished seeing all his patients now.

He checked Sam over one more time, crouching down

on the floor beside the child rather than making him get up. Anna couldn't help noticing how good he was with the little boy and how Sam responded immediately to his firm but patient approach. Ben Cole would make a wonderful father, she found herself thinking wistfully, then realised how dangerous a thought that was.

'I'm happy that what happened was simply the result of his ear infection,' Ben explained after he had finished. 'I'm going to give you a prescription for antibiotics to fight the infection and drops to soothe the inflammation in his ears. But I want you to promise me that you'll call the surgery immediately if you are at all concerned about Sam.'

'I'll do that, Doctor,' Lucy agreed, getting up. 'You don't think that he'll have another of those convulsions, do you?'

'I'm ninety-nine per cent certain that he won't as long as you keep his temperature down. But, as I said, if you're at all worried, don't hesitate to phone us.'

'I shall. Thank you.' The girl turned to Anna. 'And I'll try doing as you said and putting the drops in Sam's ears while he's sitting quietly.'

'It usually works,' Anna assured her. 'But don't worry if you have to give it a couple of goes. The more agitated you get, the more Sam will play you up.'

Sam was reluctant to leave his exciting new toys at first but he was finally persuaded that he could play with them another day. Anna followed as Ben saw them out. The waiting room was empty and Eileen had started switching off the lights now that everyone had left. The receptionist sighed ruefully when she saw Anna.

'Talk about being thrown in at the deep end! I bet you're sorry that you took this job.'

Anna laughed. 'Oh, it will take more than that to put me off. I'm far tougher than I look.'

'You'll need to be, working here,' Eileen retorted, winking at her. She pretended not to have noticed that Ben had come back into the room. 'It's not just the general public who lead you a merry dance, I'm afraid. Some members of the staff here would try the patience of a saint at times.'

'I wonder why my ears are burning? You weren't alluding to me, by any chance, were you, Eileen?' he asked wryly.

'Now, why should you think that?' the receptionist retorted. 'It wouldn't have anything to do with the fact that you told three people to make appointments for Monday morning when I'd already warned you that your list was full?'

'Sorry.' Ben tried to look contrite but his eyes were full of laughter when he turned to Anna. 'Eileen is a real termagant when it comes to her appointment system. It's a big mistake to fall foul of her, believe me. You end up having to make your own coffee for the next week!'

'I'm only trying to safeguard your interests, Dr Cole,' the receptionist said with a sniff, although Anna could tell that she wasn't really offended. It was obvious that Ben had a good relationship with the older woman.

'I know you are. And I am grateful. Honestly.' Ben gave Eileen a warm smile. 'We wouldn't be able to run this place half as efficiently without you here to keep order, Eileen.'

'Well, I don't know about that,' she said. However, it was obvious that she was pleased by the compliment. They exchanged a few more pleasantries then Eileen fetched her coat and left.

Ben sighed as the door closed. 'That's it, then. End of another busy morning. Thanks again for all your help, Anna. I really appreciate it.'

'It was nothing,' she assured him. She glanced at her watch as he went behind the desk to turn off the rest of the lights. 'Anyway, I'd better get a move on. I want to get to the shops before they close,' she explained when he turned to look at her. 'I need to stock up on groceries.'

'You didn't bring any with you?'

'I never gave it a thought, to be honest. I had too many other things on my mind.' Her face clouded as she thought about what had happened that morning. She still felt sick when she recalled what had been said…

'Are you OK?'

She jumped, feeling the colour rush to her cheeks when she saw the concern in Ben's eyes. She had a sudden urge to pour out the whole miserable story before it struck her what a mistake that would be.

She couldn't afford to tell anyone the truth just yet. Although Ben Cole had come across as both kind and sympathetic, there was no knowing how he might react. Did she really want to run the risk of losing this job?

'I'm fine. Just a bit worn out after all the rushing around,' she replied evasively.

'No wonder. As Eileen said, you were rather pushed in at the deep end.'

He smiled at her and Anna felt a flurry ripple through her when she saw the appreciation in his eyes. It was obvious that Ben found her attractive, and whilst part of her rejoiced in the fact another part knew that it would be a mistake to encourage him.

'How about if I gave you a lift into town?' he continued. 'You can get your shopping then I'll drive you back here so that you don't need to lug a lot of heavy bags. In fact, we could have some lunch first—'

'No!' She saw his start of surprise but she had to make her position clear once and for all. 'There's no easy way to say this, Dr Cole, so I may as well be blunt. I prefer to keep my private life and my professional one strictly separate.'

She shrugged, feeling a shiver working its way down her spine when she saw how he was looking at her now. There was no warmth in his gaze any longer, just a remoteness that made her heart ache in the strangest way. 'Whilst I intend to give one hundred per cent commitment during surgery hours, I'm not interested in fostering any kind of relationship with colleagues outside those times. Have I made myself clear?'

'As crystal, Miss Clemence. I apologise if I was over-stepping the mark.'

His tone crackled with ice, leaving her in little doubt that he wouldn't make the same mistake again. He switched off the last remaining lights then strode around the desk, pausing when he realised that she was still standing there. Anna had to steel herself when she caught the full force of his icy stare.

'Was there something else, Miss Clemence? If not, I'd like to set the alarm and lock up.'

'I don't appear to have a key to the back door of the flat,' she explained woodenly. 'I'll need it to get in and out over the weekend.'

'I'll see if it's in Adam's desk,' he told her curtly. He swung round, leaving Anna to follow. She was miserably aware that he was annoyed with her. Not that she blamed him, of course. She'd been rude as she'd laid down the ground rules. Her only excuse was that she'd had no choice.

'Here it is.' He offered her the key then looked steadily at her. 'Is that all now?'

'Yes.' She cleared her throat but it was an effort to force the words past the lump in it when she saw the chill in his eyes. 'Thank you.'

He inclined his head, although he didn't say anything as he strode past her. Anna watched him go into the office then turned and quickly made her way to the stairs. She was halfway up them when she heard the alarm beeping, followed a few seconds later by the sound of the front door closing. And it seemed to her that she had never felt more alone than she did at that moment.

Ben had offered her the hand of friendship and she had rejected it. Maybe she'd had no choice but it hurt to know that he wouldn't offer it to her again. It struck her all of a sudden that she would have liked to have had him for a friend, to have been able to turn to him when times became really tough.

She sighed sadly.

Would Ben Cole still want to be her friend when he found out what she had taken such care to keep secret? He would probably thank his lucky stars that he hadn't got involved!

Her hand went to the gentle swell of her stomach concealed beneath her loose fitting T-shirt and her eyes were suddenly sad.

How many men would be interested in befriending a woman who was having someone else's baby?

CHAPTER TWO

'I WONDER if you could do me a favour?'

Anna was in the treatment room when Ben Cole tapped on the door. It was Friday morning and surgery was coming to an end. It had been a busy morning as usual, but she had thoroughly enjoyed her first week in Winton. Any qualms she'd had about her ability to do the job had soon disappeared. The work might be rather different to what she was used to but the basic procedures were the same, and she really liked the people she was working with.

All in all, Anna had decided that things were working out rather better than she had feared they would. The only cloud on the horizon was the fact that Ben Cole continued to treat her with a distant courtesy that stung. Now as she saw the chilly expression on his face she had to bite back a sigh.

'Of course. What would you like me to do?' she asked politely.

'I've a patient with me who needs a blood test and I'd like to get it done as soon as possible. Would you have time to see her now, by any chance?' he asked, equally politely.

'Yes, there's no problem. I've only got one more patient to see and he hasn't arrived yet.' Anna glanced at her watch. 'In fact, if you send her straight in to see me then I should be able to catch the courier. He's due in about ten minutes to collect today's samples.'

'Fine. The lab won't have any excuse for not getting the

results back to us early next week, then.' Ben sounded re-lieved and she frowned.

'Is it that urgent?'

'Yes and no.' He sighed when he saw that she didn't understand. 'I've been trying to get this woman to have a blood test for months but each time I suggest it she finds some sort of excuse. I'm not sure what the problem is, to be honest.'

'I see. Why did she come to see you in the first place?' Anna asked curiously, thinking that it was a strange situa-tion.

'She's been suffering from night sweats and hot flushes,' he explained. 'She's in her mid-forties so I did suggest that it was probably the first sign of the menopause, but she got really upset by the idea. I'm hoping that she will accept it once we get the results of the blood test, then I can start her on HRT.'

'A lot of women find it difficult to come to terms with the fact that they are reaching that stage in their lives,' she observed softly.

'I know, and I'm sympathetic to how they feel, believe me. However, this patient seems unusually loath to accept the idea. She's so adamant, in fact, that I'm starting to wonder if I'm simply opting for the easy answer.' Ben frowned thoughtfully.

'What?' Anna asked impulsively. She gave a little shrug when he looked at her. 'I can tell that you're trying to make up your mind about something.'

He laughed and she felt a shiver run down her spine when she heard the unaccustomed warmth in his voice. 'You're far too perceptive, Anna. It wouldn't be easy to pull the wool over your eyes.'

'Oh, I'm as gullible as the next person, believe me,' she replied, feeling the tiny stab of pain that speared her heart.

She couldn't help wishing that she hadn't been quite so trusting in the past year. If she'd realised what would happen, would she have decided on the course she'd taken?

It was impossible to answer a question like that so she didn't try. She looked up, feeling a ripple of apprehension run through her when she saw how Ben was looking at her.

'That sounded as though it was spoken from the heart,' he said quietly.

'Probably.' She summoned a smile, wishing that she had hidden her feelings better. The last thing she wanted was to incite his curiosity. 'Anyway, what's the patient's name and what tests do you want done?'

'Janice Robertson. Here are her notes.' He handed her the patient's record card. 'I want the full works—cell count, proteins, gases, antibodies, micro-organisms, and so on. I don't want to overlook anything just in case I'm on the wrong track. I want to get this sorted out while I have the chance.'

'Fine. I'll get straight onto it.'

Anna turned away, making a great production out of finding everything she needed. She breathed a little sigh of relief when she heard the door closing. She really must be more careful about what she said! Ben had obviously been suspicious just now and she didn't want him wondering what she had to hide.

She sighed again as she took a couple of fresh vials out of a drawer for the blood samples. She was going to have to tell people about the baby at some point. Although she had managed to disguise her pregnancy so far, the time was fast approaching when she wouldn't be able to hide it any longer. She couldn't help worrying how the staff at the surgery were going to react when they found out. Would they be angry that she hadn't told them before? She really couldn't blame them if they were.

It was a sobering thought but she tried not to dwell on it as she got ready. When Janice Robertson tapped on the door a few minutes later she had everything set up.

'Come in,' she called, smiling reassuringly as the woman hesitantly entered the room. 'Hello, there. I'm Anna Clemence, the new practice nurse. Dr Cole wants you to have a blood test, I believe?'

'That's right.'

Anna frowned when she heard the reluctance in the other woman's voice. She couldn't help noticing how dejected the woman looked as she ushered her to a chair. It was obvious that Janice wasn't keen to have the test done, although, like Ben, Anna wasn't sure what the problem was.

'I've got everything ready so you just make yourself comfortable. Have you ever had a blood test before?' she asked soothingly, picking up the webbing strap that she would use as a tourniquet while she took the sample. Maybe Janice was frightened of needles and that was why she looked so upset. She'd seen enough grown men keel over to know how the sight of a syringe could affect some people!

'Only when I was pregnant.' Janice suddenly smiled so that her whole face lit up. 'They were *always* taking blood from me then!'

'I can imagine!' Anna laughed, although it was hard to hide her amazement at the transformation in the woman. 'There's all sorts of things that need to be checked when you're having a baby. I bet you got fed up with all the tests.'

'Oh, I didn't mind,' Janice assured her. 'I mean, you don't, do you? Not when it's to make sure that your baby's going to be healthy.'

'No, of course not. That's the most important thing, isn't it?' Anna replied, thinking how very true that was. She tightened the tourniquet around Janice's arm then picked up the syringe. 'Now, all you'll feel is a little scratch. It won't really hurt so don't worry.'

She deftly inserted the needle into the vein then started to draw off a small amount of blood. 'How many children do you have, by the way?' she asked to distract her. Although Janice didn't appear to be worried about what was happening, it seemed safer to keep her talking.

'Two, a boy and a girl. Susan and Richard.' Janice sighed heavily. 'They're both grown up now, of course. Richard works in London and Susan is taking a gap year between finishing university and finding a job. She's in Australia at the moment.'

Anna snapped the end off the vial and quickly filled in the label with the patient's name, address, date of birth and the address code for the surgery. She picked up a second vial, knowing that the lab would require two samples to complete all the tests Ben had requested.

'You must miss them,' she observed, drawing off the second vial of blood.

'I do. The house seems so empty without them. I don't know what to do with myself most days. Alan—that's my husband—is always at work, you see. He's a builder and he has his own business. He's been so busy recently that he's gone from early morning until late at night. I'm on my own most of the time and it gets very lonely.'

Janice tried to smile but Anna could see the tears that had welled into her eyes. She frowned as she pressed a small adhesive dressing over the puncture mark in the crook of the woman's elbow.

Could it be that some of Janice's problems stemmed from loneliness? she wondered. Ben had seemed to think that it was more than just the physical signs of the meno-pause that were troubling her so it just seemed to fit.

Although loneliness wasn't an illness in itself, it often led to depression and that could cause a variety of symptoms ranging from mild anxiety to hallucinations in extreme cases.

'It must do,' Anna said sympathetically, making a note to mention it to him. 'When you've been used to rushing around, looking after a family, it must be strange to have all that free time on your hands. Do you go out to work?'

'No. I always stayed at home to look after the children. Alan's business has done very well so we didn't need the extra money, and he's never liked the idea of me working. Anyway, I can't see anyone wanting to employ me now, not at my age and with no real experience to offer.'

'How about voluntary work?' Anna suggested thoughtfully. It was obvious that staying in the house on her own all day wasn't doing Janice any good, and there had to be a solution. 'A lot of charities are crying out for people to help them. Or what about helping out at the local playgroup? I'm sure they'd be thrilled to have someone with your experience.'

'Do you think so?' Janice said eagerly. 'I'd never given it a thought, to be honest, but it would be lovely to be around small children again. I loved it when my two were toddlers. It was the happiest time of my life.'

'I'm almost certain there's a notice on the board in the foyer for the local playgroup,' Anna told her, delighted to see the woman looking so much more animated. 'Why don't we take a look? There might be a phone number you could call. You could have a chat with whoever runs the group and see how they would feel about you helping.'

She led the way through the waiting room, holding open the door while Janice followed her into the foyer. The notice-board was covered with posters advertising various events that were due to take place in the town but she soon spotted the one she wanted.

'There it is. And they've given the name and the telephone number of the lady who runs the playgroup. I'll just fetch a pen and some paper then you can jot down the details.'

Anna hurried back inside and went straight to the reception desk. Eileen had just finished taking a phone call and she looked up when Anna approached her. 'Problems?'

'Not really. I just need a pen and a scrap of paper if you've got one handy.'

Eileen found them for her. 'Anything else?'

'No, that's fine. Thanks,' Anna assured her. She went back to the foyer and quickly noted down the details for Janice then handed her the slip of paper. 'Now, promise me that you'll give them a call. There's no point letting your talents go to waste.'

Janice laughed delightedly. 'Oh, wouldn't it be wonderful if they said I could help out? I'll phone them as soon as I get home.'

'You do that,' Anna agreed, smiling to herself as she watched her leave. The difference in Janice's demeanour was simply amazing, she thought.

'What have you been doing to make Janice Robertson look so cheerful all of a sudden?'

She swung round when she heard Ben's voice, feeling a little flurry run through her when she found him standing in the doorway. 'I just suggested that she should contact the local playgroup and see if they need any volunteers to help them.' She quickly repeated what the woman had told her. 'I got the impression that she was lonely and thought that this might be just what she needed.'

'I see.' He suddenly smiled at her. 'Maybe I should ask you for help more often.'

Anna laughed but she couldn't deny how good it felt to have him looking at her without that awful chill in his eyes for once. It struck her how much it had hurt to have him treat her so distantly all week.

'I'm only too happy to help any time I can,' she assured him huskily, rather surprised by the idea.

Ben took a deep breath and even as she watched the warmth faded from his face. 'So long as it's within working hours and strictly inside the terms of your contract, of course.'

She shrugged, feeling deeply hurt that he should have seen fit to remind her at that precise moment about what she had said. 'I don't imagine I'm any different to you or Adam in that respect. We all need a life outside working hours.'

'I'm sure you're right.' His tone was cool now. 'Anyway, well done. I've had my suspicions that Janice was suffering from mild depression as much as anything else. Let's hope that your idea has done the trick. Sometimes all it needs is for a person to be pointed in the right direction.'

He went back inside and she saw him go over to speak to Eileen. Anna heard the receptionist laugh at something he said as she went back into the waiting room, but she didn't go over to find out what the joke was. She doubted if Ben would have wanted to share it with her, anyway.

That thought hurt far more than it should have done. Anna deliberately put it out of her mind as she went back to her room and packed up the samples ready for collection. The courier arrived a short time later, closely followed by her last patient, so she had no time to brood.

The rest of the day flew past with barely a minute to breathe, let alone worry about anything other than making sure that she did everything right. However, as she got ready for bed that night Anna found herself thinking about what Ben had said to her.

Maybe it was her imagination but there had seemed to be a hint of regret in Ben's voice as he'd reminded her of her decision to keep her working life and her professional one strictly separate. If she hadn't known better, she might even think that he was hurt rather angry about her refusal to have lunch with him the previous week.

She rolled over and closed her eyes, willing the thought from her mind. She didn't like to think of Ben being hurt, funnily enough.

Saturday arrived and Anna got up early. She had the flat cleaned and her washing done by eleven o'clock. She decided that she would go into town and do some shopping because she'd bought only the barest necessities the previous week.

She sighed as she found her thoughts immediately returning to Ben once again—she had to stop thinking about him all the time! She had made the right decision and there was no point harping on about it. She would be polite and friendly within the limits of their working relationship, but that was all. There was no point in wishing that she had handled things differently and certainly no point in wishing that she hadn't rebuffed him!

She slipped on a lightweight jacket over her jeans and T-shirt then left the flat. The forecast was for rain later in the day but she was planning on being back well before then. She ran down the steps but paused when she saw Adam Knight, the senior partner, crossing the car park.

'End of another busy week,' he commented, stopping to speak to her. 'How have you enjoyed it, Anna? It's not been too big a change for you?'

Anna smiled when she saw the kindly concern on his

face. She had spoken to Adam several times during the week and had found him extremely helpful on each occasion. He had a quiet confidence and authority that inspired respect in everyone who came into contact with him. She found herself thinking how like Ben he was in that regard before she realised where her thoughts were wandering once more.

'I've really enjoyed it,' she said quickly, focusing firmly on the conversation. 'It's been a bit strange at times but the routine procedures are the same wherever you work.'

'Well, I have to say that we've been very glad to have you here. I was saying to Ben yesterday that we would have been hard pressed to cope if you hadn't taken the job.' Adam smiled warmly at her. 'We were extremely fortunate to get someone of your calibre for the post.'

'I was glad to be offered it,' she said sincerely, although she couldn't help feeling guilty. She was very much aware of how differently Adam might feel when he found out that she was pregnant. Maybe she hadn't been obliged to tell him before she had accepted the job, but most employers would have expected to have been told in advance. It was just that she had been so desperate to get the job that she had felt that she'd had no choice.

She took a deep breath, wondering if it would be best to tell him now and get it over with. Adam had had a week to see that she was capable of doing the work so surely that would go in her favour? Even though he might be upset about her oversight, she didn't think from what she knew of him that he would go so far as to sack her.

Would he?

It was that last thought which made her hesitate, and before she could make up her mind what to do he glanced at his watch.

'I'd better get a move on. I've had strict instructions not

to be late.' He grimaced. 'Beth has invited my aunt and uncle to stay for the weekend and she wants me there to give her a hand, getting everything ready. You'd think we had royalty visiting from all the preparations she's been making!'

Anna smiled at his wry tone, hating herself for feeling so relieved at having an excuse to put off her confession a little longer. 'I expect she wants everything to be just right.'

'So she keeps telling me,' he agreed drolly, then suddenly smiled. 'Actually, things couldn't be any more perfect. I didn't know what I'd been missing all my life until I met Beth.'

Anna sighed as he sketched her a wave and got into his car. It must be wonderful to feel like that about someone, to love and be loved in return, to have someone beside you to face all life's problems. Unbidden, a picture of Ben Cole's handsome face sprang to mind and she frowned. Why on earth had she thought about Ben in that context?

It was all very strange but she tried not to think about it as she walked into town. She went straight to the supermarket but it was crowded with shoppers that day. It took her far longer than she'd expected to collect what she needed then she had to wait ages in the queue at the checkout. By the time she left the store, there were huge black clouds gathering overhead and the first few spots of rain were starting to fall.

Anna sighed as she took a firmer grip on the heavy carrier bags. She would have dearly loved to have taken a taxi but she simply didn't have the money for that kind of luxury. It looked as though she was going to get very, very wet!

She was halfway home when the heavens opened and the rain started to fall with a vengeance. She stopped and looked around for somewhere to shelter. She spotted the entrance to the park and wondered fleetingly if there might be somewhere there where she could wait out the storm. However, she soon decided that it would be a waste of time going to take a look when she saw a jogger running briskly out of the gates. Surely even the most ardent keep-fit fanatic wouldn't *choose* to run round in a torrential downpour if there was anywhere to shelter!

She had set off again, moving closer to the wall, when she heard footsteps pounding along the pavement behind her. Having her head bowed against the rain, she didn't notice the runner drawing alongside her. She nearly jumped out of her skin when a familiar voice spoke in her ear.

'Here, give me some of those bags. It will be quicker if we both carry them.'

She swung round, unable to hide her surprise when she saw who it was. 'Ben! What are you doing here?'

'I certainly wasn't following you, if that's what you're wondering. I happened to see you as I came out of the park.' He gave her a grim smile and she felt herself flush.

'I never thought you were following me,' she denied hotly, glaring at him, then felt her anger get hijacked along the way when she suddenly realised what he was wearing, which was remarkably little, quite frankly.

Anna took a deep breath but it was impossible to control the sudden lurch her pulse gave as her eyes swept down the length of his body. The outfit that Ben had on was perfectly appropriate for what he had been doing. However, there was little doubt in her mind that the sight of his muscular body clad only in those brief, black running shorts and vest would have had an effect on even the sternest female heart!

She quickly averted her gaze, terrified that he would guess what was going through her mind. She wasn't a prude by any means, but was it really right to have been dwelling on the length and shape of his powerful legs with such *enjoyment*? Should she have been deriving such *pleasure* from studying the narrowness of his hips and waist? Or gaining so much *satisfaction* from gazing at those gleaming wet pectoral muscles? She didn't think so!

'Come on, Anna. Do you want a hand with those bags or not? It's up to you.'

She blinked when she heard the impatience in his voice. 'I…hum…'

It was on the tip of her tongue to refuse when Ben took the decision from her. 'We'll both end up with pneumonia if we stand here much longer while you try to decide if you can trust me,' he snapped, taking most of the shopping bags from her.

'Trust you?' she said uncertainly.

'Uh-huh.' He held up his hand as though he were swearing an oath. 'I promise on my honour that this isn't a ploy to get you back to your flat and have my wicked way with you. I just wanted to help you, although I'm beginning to wish that I'd curbed my Boy Scout instincts.'

Anna blushed hotly. The worst thing was that she couldn't think of a word to say in her own defence. Fortunately, Ben didn't wait around to hear her reply. He set off up the road at a fast lope, leaving her to trail after him, miserably aware that she had made a fool of herself. Even though she hadn't imagined for a second that he had been planning to have his 'wicked way' with her, there was no way on earth that she could have explained what had been going through her mind!

They walked back to the flat in total silence. Ben kept a couple of steps ahead of her all the way, giving her no opportunity to say anything even if she'd wanted to. He paused at the bottom of the steps leading up to the flat.

'Leave the shopping here and I'll bring it up. You go and unlock the door.'

Anna just managed to stop herself saluting when she heard the imperious note in his voice. However, it didn't seem worth promoting an argument. She ran up the steps and opened the door, moving aside so that he could carry the shopping bags inside.

He plonked them on the kitchen table then turned to leave. 'That's it, then. I'll see you on Monday.'

'Wait!' Anna didn't know where that word had sprung from. She certainly hadn't been intending to say it. She shrugged when he looked at her, seeing the chill in his dark eyes, and couldn't help wishing that she could do something to repair the damage that she had caused the previous Saturday, but she didn't know how to go about it.

'Thank you for helping me,' she said instead, falling back on good manners when all else had failed. 'I really appreciate it.'

'You're welcome.' There was slightly less coolness in his voice now but she couldn't decide if it was due to her apology or to the shiver that had racked him. She frowned when she saw the goose-bumps that had broken out all over his skin.

'You're absolutely freezing!' she exclaimed in concern.

'I'll live.' He turned towards the door once again but Anna knew that she couldn't let him leave. It was pouring down with rain and, from the look of the sky, likely to keep on doing so for some time to come. She couldn't in all conscience let him go home in weather like that.

'Look, why don't you wait here until the rain slackens off a bit? It's stupid getting soaked when you don't have to.'

'I doubt if I could get any wetter,' he observed so wryly that she laughed.

Her gaze whizzed down his body and she felt a ripple of pure sexual awareness run through her when she saw how the wet clothes were clinging to his muscular body.

'Maybe not,' she said quickly, hoping that he couldn't tell how shocked she felt. She wasn't totally naïve. She'd been in a relationship before she'd left London and had enjoyed the physical side as much as the companionship, but she'd never expected to feel this kind of sexual awareness towards any man in her condition. 'But it's silly to go back out into that storm when there's no need. How about if I make some coffee to warm us both up? I'm sure you could do with a cup as much as I could.'

'Well, if you're sure....' He hesitated a moment then shrugged. 'Fine. Coffee sounds good. I must confess that I could do with something to take the chill out of my bones.'

He shivered again and she sighed. 'It's going to take more than a cup of coffee to do that. You need to get out of those wet clothes for a start.'

She hurried on when she sensed that he was going to object, knowing that she would never forgive herself if he ended up making himself ill when he had been trying to help her. 'Why don't you have a hot shower while the coffee's brewing? I've got an old tracksuit somewhere about that's way too big for me. It might just fit you. I can put your clothes in the dryer while we wait for the rain to stop.'

'That's kind of you, Anna, but I don't want to be a nuisance,' he said levelly. But she knew what he'd really meant. Ben didn't want to overstep the boundaries she had set in place, and her heart ached because she couldn't help wishing that it hadn't been necessary to instigate them in the first place.

'It's no trouble,' she assured him quietly. She turned away to plug in the kettle, afraid that he would see that she was upset. 'You go and take that shower. I'll leave the tracksuit outside the bathroom door for you.'

She breathed a sigh of relief when she heard him leaving the room. Maybe it was silly but Ben *disturbed* her. She didn't know why, she just knew that he did. He made her feel things that she hadn't expected to feel and she wasn't sure how to deal with them.

Anna closed her mind to that thought, afraid of where it might lead to. She made the coffee then left it in the cafetière to brew and went to find the tracksuit for him. She put it on the floor outside the bathroom door then went back to her bedroom. Although the jacket had saved her from getting completely soaked through, her jeans were sodden and she needed to change them.

She stripped them off and draped them over the back of a chair to dry then picked up a brush to tidy her hair. It was months since she'd had it cut and it reached way past her shoulders now. She fastened it up into a ponytail with a bright green elasticated bobble then grimaced when she caught sight of herself in the dressing-table mirror. She couldn't help thinking how at odds the youthful hairstyle was with her burgeoning figure.

She turned sideways to the mirror, pulling the baggy T-shirt taut across the full swell of her breasts and the pronounced curve of her belly. Day by day her body was changing as the baby grew. In one way it was exciting to see the evidence of what was happening but in another it was scary. She couldn't help wondering how she would feel as her pregnancy advanced. Would she feel proud of the new life growing inside her or simply ugly when her body became even more swollen?

'Thanks for the tracksuit. Not quite the perfect fit, shall we say...'

Anna's head swung round and she felt a wave of sickness

hit her when she saw Ben standing in the doorway. At any other time she might have found the sight of him standing there with his muscular arms and legs poking out of her tracksuit amusing. However, she had absolutely no desire to laugh when she saw the dawning shock that crossed his face.

She let go of the T-shirt abruptly so that its concealing folds hid her stomach from view, but the damage had been done. Ben had obviously guessed that she was pregnant. She could tell that from the way he was looking at her.

'We need to talk, Anna. I'll wait in the kitchen for you.'

He turned and strode away but for a few seconds she didn't move. She closed her eyes, remembering how he'd looked at her. There was no doubt that he had been shocked and she could understand that. She also could understand if he was angry about her deception. But how would he feel when he found out the truth about this baby? Would he be repulsed by what she had done?

She knew that a lot of people would find what she had done totally unacceptable. She had already encountered disapproval, in fact, and from the least expected sources, yet the thought that Ben might feel the same filled her with dread.

She could deal with his shock, cope with his anger, but she couldn't bear it if he was *disgusted*!

Anna opened her eyes and looked at herself in the mirror. She simply couldn't bear it.

CHAPTER THREE

'I DIDN'T know if you took sugar.'

'I don't. Thank you.' Anna sat down at the table and wrapped her hands around the cup Ben had placed in front of her. Her fingers felt numb with cold but even the heat from the coffee couldn't seem to warm them.

Ben had had the coffee poured by the time she'd reached the kitchen. He had found the milk in one of the carrier bags and a jug to put it in, even emptied some sugar into a bowl. Now, as he sat down opposite her, she felt a little bubble of hysteria floating to the surface of her mind. Were they really going to sit here, politely drinking coffee, while they discussed what he had seen?

She pushed back her chair in a sudden fit of impatience. Striding to the window, she stared out at the rain for a moment then spun round to face him. She wasn't sure exactly why she was so angry all of a sudden but there was no point in prolonging the agony.

'I'm pregnant. You obviously gathered that from what you saw just now. The only thing I need to know now is if it is going to make any difference to me working here.'

Ben took a sip of coffee then put his cup down carefully on a table mat. 'I assume that Adam doesn't know?'

'No. I deliberately didn't tell him.' She stared defiantly back at him, refusing to let him think that she was ashamed of what she had done.

'I take it that you had a reason?' he said levelly.

'The best reason in the world—I desperately needed this job,' she shot back, wondering why his calmness stung so much. She would almost have preferred him to speak angrily to her, to show any kind of emotion rather than that icy detachment.

'I see. Would I be right to assume that the baby's father is no longer on the scene?'

'Yes.' She gave a brittle laugh, feeling the pain welling up inside her. 'He has made it abundantly clear that he doesn't intend to be around when this child is born so you can safely count him out.'

'There are ways of making a man support his child financially,' he said flatly. He picked up his cup again and she was shocked to see that his hands were shaking. It made her realise that his apparent calmness was an act and that inside he didn't feel at all calm about what had happened.

'I know there are,' she said more quietly, shocked by the discovery. 'However, I have no intention of asking him for money. I'll manage by myself.'

'You say that now but what about after the baby is born? How are you going to manage then?' He slammed his cup back on the mat, seemingly uncaring that coffee slopped onto the table. 'Principles are all well and good, Anna, but they won't feed you. They won't put a roof over your head or pay the bills. This child didn't ask to be born. The least you can do is make sure that he or she is properly taken care of!'

His anger rose on a great wave, startling her by its speed and ferocity, and she blinked. 'Of course I shall! Look, Ben, my main concern is the baby's welfare. I will do anything and everything in my power to make sure that it is well cared for.'

'So why won't you make the father share some of the responsibility?' he bit out. 'All right, so maybe you've had some sort of disagreement with him, but surely you can find a way round it? You must have felt something for the guy otherwise you wouldn't be in this situation!'

'It's not that simple.' Anna could feel the heat warming her cheeks and looked away. Ben's reaction had shaken her because it seemed too...*personal*, if that was the right word. 'It isn't just a question of making him accept responsibility.'

'Why not?' he demanded harshly, then suddenly stopped. Anna felt a shiver race through her. She couldn't recall having seen such contempt on anyone's face before. She was still trying to work out what had caused him to look at her like that when he continued, and she felt sick when she heard the disdain in his voice.

'He's married, isn't he? That's why he doesn't want anything to do with you and the child.'

She took a deep breath, forcing the nausea to subside to a level she could deal with. Ben wasn't looking at her now. He was staring at his coffee and it was impossible to tell what he was thinking, which was a relief. It wasn't nice to know that he thought her capable of having an affair with a married man!

'No, he isn't married,' she replied hollowly. 'His wife is dead. She died a month ago.'

He looked up, a frown drawing his brows into a straight line. 'Around the same time as your sister died? Didn't you tell me that it was a month ago that it happened?'

'That's right.' Suddenly Anna knew that there was no point prevaricating any longer. She had to tell him the truth even though the thought of how he might react scared her.

She sat down again, wondering why it should matter what he thought. Ben's opinion wasn't going to change anything; it certainly wouldn't make any difference to the situation. Nevertheless, she knew in her heart that she wanted him to understand and not think too badly of her.

'Jo died a month ago, a month after I found out that I was pregnant. She was so pleased. I don't think I have ever seen anyone who was so thrilled.' She felt her eyes fill with tears and quickly blinked them away, knowing that she couldn't afford to break down before she had told him the whole story. Ben didn't say a word, leaving her to do all the talking, and in a way that made it easier. She would deal with his reaction later and simply concentrate on telling him the facts for now.

'Jo always wanted a family, you see. She used to say that she'd been born into the wrong era because she wasn't interested in having a career. All she ever longed for was a child to love and care for.'

'Did she have problems conceiving because of her cancer?' Ben asked quietly when she paused.

Anna nodded. 'Yes. She couldn't understand it at first. She and Mike decided to try for a baby as soon as they got married but it just didn't happen. In the end, Jo went for tests and that was when they discovered that she had endometrial cancer.' Her hands clenched around the cup as she recalled that painful time.

'So what happened?' he prompted, still in that same quiet tone that somehow seemed to make it easier to continue.

'She was told that she would need a total hysterectomy, and have her Fallopian tubes and ovaries removed as well. At that point the doctors weren't sure how far the cancer had spread but they were hopeful that they would be able to contain it.

'Jo was devastated when she found out. I think she was more upset because she would no longer be able to have children than because she had cancer. That was when I decided that I had to help her.' She faltered as she reached the really difficult bit in the story.

'What exactly are you saying, Anna?' He laid his hand

on the table, palm up, and it seemed to her that she had never heard such gentleness in anyone's voice before. 'Tell me.'

She took a deep breath then slowly unclenched her hand and placed it in his, feeling the ripple that ran through her when she felt his fingers closing around hers. 'That I offered to have a baby for her.'

'Are you saying that you're a surrogate for your sister? Is that it?'

She heard the shock in his voice and sighed. 'Yes, that's exactly what I'm saying. The surgeons agreed to harvest some of Jo's eggs when they operated on her. I think it was the only thing that kept her going, to be honest. The thought that one day she might hold her own child in her arms gave her the incentive to get better.'

'And her husband agreed to it?' he asked quietly.

'Oh, yes. We wouldn't have gone ahead if Mike hadn't said that it was what he wanted, too. We certainly wouldn't have been able to find a clinic willing to help us if he had been opposed to the idea because it was his sperm that was going to be used to fertilise Jo's eggs. As it was, we ended up going privately because none of the NHS clinics we approached could help us.'

'Because of your sister's health?'

'That wasn't a problem, actually. There are guidelines about which women can be offered treatment by *in vitro* fertilisation surrogacy and hysterectomy for cancer is one of the recognised medical conditions. The real obstacle was funding. There are so many people requiring fertility treatment that there simply isn't enough money to go round.' She shrugged. 'Some clinics prefer not to go down the surrogacy route.'

Ben sighed. 'There's still a lot of opposition to surrogacy. I can understand the concerns, of course, but in a case like this…well.'

. He shrugged, making his views on the subject clear. Anna felt a little more of her tension melt away. It made it that bit easier to tell him the rest of the story—the worst bit, to her mind.

'Anyway, once we had found a clinic willing to help us we all had to have lengthy counselling to make sure that we understood the pitfalls of what we were planning. As I mentioned, there are guidelines laid down and the whole business is strictly regulated.'

'Sensible. I've read a number of reports about intended parents and surrogates falling out after the baby was born,' Ben commented.

'Exactly. Then there was a six-month wait, a kind of quarantine period, you could call it, while the embryos were checked for HIV infection. Once that was completed, and Jo's doctors had submitted a report on her health, our case was put before the ethics committee.'

'It would have gone against you if there had been any doubts about your sister's long-term health at that stage?' Ben queried curiously.

'Oh, yes. Our case wouldn't have been passed and we would never have been allowed to proceed,' she explained. 'Fortunately, Jo appeared to have responded to the treatment, so there was no problem there. We'd been warned that we might need a couple of attempts before anything happened but, in the event, I got pregnant first time. Jo was ecstatic. You can't imagine how happy she was when I told her the news.'

'How about her husband? Mike, was it?'

'He *said* he was pleased, although I had a feeling that he was only saying it to keep Jo happy. I probably would have made him tell me what was wrong, only a week after

I found out I was pregnant Jo was taken ill again. The cancer had spread to her liver. I think she'd had an inkling that something had been wrong for a while, but she hadn't said anything because she was afraid that we would be refused treatment if there were fresh doubts about her health. It turned out that the cancer was too advanced for them to do anything and she died a month later.'

'That must have been rough for you, especially in the circumstances,' he said gently, squeezing her hand.

'It was.' She smiled sadly. 'The one thing that kept me going was the thought of the baby. I was certain that Mike would feel the same but I was completely wrong about that. It turned out that he'd been having an affair with a woman he worked with. I'm not sure why he hadn't told Jo what was going on. I suppose he felt guilty after what she'd been through. However, he was perfectly clear about what he intended to do after the funeral.'

'And what was that?'

'He told me that he no longer wanted the baby, that he and this woman were planning on moving to America and they didn't want a child cluttering up their lives. With the money from the sale of the house, plus what he received from Jo's life insurance policy, they'd have enough to set themselves up. So far as Mike was concerned, it was up to me whether or not I kept the baby. He didn't want anything more to do with it.'

'It must have been a tough decision for you to make,' he said bluntly.

'Funnily enough, it wasn't. I knew straight away what I was going to do.' She gripped Ben's hand, drawing strength from the feel of it. 'I was having this baby for Jo and now it's all I have left of her. That's why I will do everything in my power to make sure that it's loved and cared for. This is Jo's baby as well as mine!'

Ben didn't say anything for a moment. Anna frowned because it was impossible to tell what he was thinking as he sat there, staring at their linked hands. She had a feeling that the story had touched him on a level she had never expected it to, yet she didn't understand why it should have had such an effect.

He suddenly looked up and she steeled herself when she saw the searching look he gave her. 'You're absolutely certain about what you're doing, Anna? It isn't too late for you to change your mind. Nobody would blame you if you did. Bringing up a child on your own isn't something to be undertaken lightly.'

She frowned when she heard the grating note in his voice. 'I know it isn't. I know it won't be easy...'

'Do you? Are you sure?' His tone was harsher than ever, the expression in his eyes making a shiver work its way down her spine. 'Maybe you *think* that you'll be able to manage, but the reality of what you're planning could turn out to be vastly different. Your whole life will be irreversibly altered, Anna. Do you understand that?'

'Of course I do!' she replied hotly, hurt that he should believe it necessary to point that out to her. She withdrew her hand abruptly, needing to stand firm in the face of his opposition. It was strange how much it hurt to have him doubt her.

'I know what I'm doing, Ben, and I won't change my mind, no matter what you or anyone else says. Maybe things haven't worked out how Jo and I planned they would, but it isn't the baby's fault. I can't just get rid of it because it's no longer *convenient* for me to have it!'

'So long as you have thought everything through,' he said flatly, but she could hear the doubt that lingered in his voice.

'I have,' she said, wanting to convince him. 'I know how difficult it will be but I'm prepared for that, I assure you.'

'I hope so, but I know from experience how hard life will be for you, Anna.' He smiled grimly when she looked at him. 'My mother was a single parent. I know how she had to struggle to bring me up.'

'I didn't know—' She broke off, realising that there was no reason why she should have known. It certainly explained why he had doubts about what she had decided to do, although she wasn't sure if that made her feel better or worse.

'Anyway, I can't begin to imagine what you must have been through in the past few weeks. It would have been bad enough coping with your sister's death without everything else on top of that.'

She glanced up as he smoothly steered the conversation away from himself. She had a feeling that he hadn't intended to tell her about his own circumstances, and didn't feel that it would be right to question him even though she was curious to learn more.

'It's been a nightmare and I don't mind admitting it,' she said softly. 'The worst thing of all was knowing that I had to find a job and somewhere to live. I'd moved in with Jo after I came back from London, you see. It made more sense than me finding a place of my own when she needed looking after.'

'Surely your brother-in-law didn't ask you to move out?' Ben demanded incredulously.

'I couldn't have stayed there,' she explained flatly. 'Mike put the house up for sale straight after the funeral and he found a buyer for it within a week. He went to stay with his girlfriend, which made the situation a bit easier. I didn't see him again until the day I moved out.' She shivered as she recalled that last dreadful scene.

Ben frowned heavily. 'What happened? Come on, Anna, tell me.'

She took a deep breath because it was difficult to talk about it. Just recalling the cruel things her brother-in-law had said made her feel sick. 'Mike came back as I was waiting for the taxi to arrive. He was…well, unpleasant.'

'In what way?' Ben demanded when she paused.

'H-he told me that if I named him as the baby's father he would deny it, and that if I ever tried to claim maintenance from him I would regret it,' she whispered brokenly. 'He said that by the time he had finished there wouldn't be a hospital in the country that would employ me. He meant it, too.'

'Hell!' Ben got up and strode to the window then swung round, anger darkening his expression. 'Not content with abdicating from his responsibilities, he saw fit to threaten you as well. Not that he would have a leg to stand on if you did decide to sue for maintenance, Anna. It doesn't take much to prove conclusively who a child's father is nowadays, thanks to DNA testing!'

'I know. But I have no intention of asking him for anything,' she said quickly. She frowned when she saw the anger on his face. Ben seemed to have taken what she had told him to heart, and it bothered her. 'Why are you so angry, Ben? I don't understand.'

He shrugged and even as she watched the shutters seemed to come down. 'Who wouldn't be angry after hearing a tale like that?'

She bit back a sigh because she knew that he was being deliberately evasive. However, at the end of the day, what did it really matter? Surely she should be more concerned about whether or not she still had a job.

She took a deep breath then hurried on before her courage deserted her.

'How is this going to affect my job at the surgery? I know it was wrong not to tell Adam at my interview, but I was desperate, you understand.'

'I do, and I don't think that you need worry too much.' Ben said firmly. 'I imagine that Adam will be a bit surprised but I can't see him sacking you, if that's what you're afraid of. It isn't the sort of thing he would do.'

She let out a heartfelt sigh of relief. 'Oh, am I glad to hear that! I don't know what I would do if I lost this job.'

He grimaced when he heard the catch in her voice. 'You must have been living on a knife edge for weeks, Anna. I can't imagine how you've coped.'

'I had no choice,' she replied flatly. 'I've no family now that Jo is dead so I just had to get on with it.'

'How about friends? Surely they would have wanted to help you?'

'I lost touch with most of my friends after I moved back here.' She shrugged. 'I was too busy nursing Jo at first to go up and down to London to see them. Then, once I'd decided that I would have the baby, it didn't seem right to contact them.'

'Why not?' he asked, frowning.

'Because I didn't want them thinking that I was expecting them to help me. I made this decision and it's up to me to see it through. I was also worried about what they would think.'

'About you being a surrogate mother, you mean?' he said astutely.

'Yes.' She looked him straight in the eye although her heart was racing. Ben had been sympathetic so far but she needed to know how he *really* felt about this situation.

'I was advised by the clinic that it might be best not to tell too many people the truth about the baby. They explained that a lot of folk might be shocked by the idea of me being a surrogate mother.' She bit her lip. 'They were right, too. When I happened to mention it at the hospital when I went for my first antenatal check-up, the nurse who was taking my blood pressure made no secret of the fact that she found the idea completely disgusting.'

'Then she shouldn't be doing the job.' Ben's tone was grim. 'Obviously it's your decision entirely what you tell people, but I can't see why anyone should be shocked or disgusted by such an unselfish act.'

He sat down and took hold of her hand again, and she shivered when she felt his fingers closing around hers. 'I think you're a very brave woman, Anna Clemence, brave and totally unselfish to do what you've done.'

'Thank you,' she whispered, feeling tears of relief welling into her eyes.

Ben sighed when he saw them. 'Hey, come on now. You'll make me feel guilty if you start crying!'

'Sorry!' She managed a watery smile as she got up and tore off a piece of kitchen roll and blew her nose. 'I'm just so relieved.'

'Relieved?'

She heard the surprise in his voice and wished that she hadn't said that. 'I was afraid that you'd be disgusted as well when you found out the truth. It wasn't only the nurse who showed how repulsive she found the idea, you see. My brother-in-law told me last week that he couldn't understand why any woman would have agreed to be a surrogate. He said that the whole idea was revolting.'

Ben's face darkened with anger. 'If he felt like that then why the hell did he agree to it in the first place?' He sighed when she didn't answer. He got up and crossed the room. Taking hold of her by the shoulders, he gave her a gentle shake.

'It sounds to me as though he was looking for an excuse

for his own despicable actions, Anna. He knew damn well that he was in the wrong, but was trying to vindicate himself by blaming you. What you've done isn't something to be ashamed of. You should be proud of yourself—do you hear me?'

'Yes.' She heard the sincerity in his voice and it felt as though a huge weight had been lifted off her shoulders all of a sudden. Ben wasn't shocked or disgusted and it felt so wonderful to know that. Her heart seemed to swell with relief as she smiled at him. 'Yes!'

The strangest expression crossed his face. Anna tensed when she felt his fingers tighten. For a dizzying moment she thought that he was going to draw her into his arms but he abruptly let her go.

'So what do you intend to do now? My advice is to tell Adam as soon as possible. Apart from any other consideration, he needs to know for your own safety.'

'My safety?' she repeated blankly. If Ben *had* pulled her into his arms, what would have happened next? a small voice was whispering. Would he have kissed her? Would she have responded?

She had no idea. However, the fact that she was even thinking about it shook her to the depths of her soul. She was over three months pregnant, for heaven's sake. She shouldn't be standing there, wondering about things like that!

'It's essential that you don't come into contact with anyone suffering from an infectious illness that might affect your baby,' he explained firmly.

'I've had German measles,' she assured him, dragging her wayward thoughts back into line.

'That's good to hear but there are other things, like chickenpox, for instance. That can seriously affect a woman in the later stages of pregnancy and cause problems for her baby.'

Anna frowned. 'But surely Adam could decide that it's not worth the risk of letting me stay on in the job?'

'I'm certain that he won't do any such thing. A lot of women continue to work in medicine while they are pregnant. It's merely a question of taking a few simple precautions,' he said firmly.

She summoned a smile but she couldn't claim that she was totally reassured. She'd been at the surgery barely a week so why should Adam feel that he should keep her on when it was going to cause him so much trouble?

'Stop it,' Ben said emphatically. He shook his head when she looked at him in surprise. 'You were worrying about what Adam is going to say and there's no need, believe me. He's one of the most sympathetic people I've ever worked with.'

'How did you know what I was thinking?' she asked in surprise.

'Because hiding your feelings isn't something you're particularly good at, Anna.'

She frowned when she heard the odd note in his voice. Ben's mouth compressed when he saw her bewilderment. 'You were polite when you turned down my invitation to lunch last Saturday, but it was obvious how much you hated the idea.'

She looked away because she wasn't sure what he might see on her face at that moment. 'I thought it was for the best, Ben. I'm only going to be here for four months or so, so there's no point me getting too…too friendly with the people I work with.'

'So you think it's best if you go it alone?' he asked levelly.

She nodded. 'I have to learn to cope by myself. At the

end of the day, this baby is my responsibility and nobody else's.'

'I understand that. But everyone needs friends to help them from time to time.' He looked at her steadily. 'I hope you'll let me be your friend, Anna.' He held his hand out to her once again. 'How about it?'

Anna stared at his hand. It was large and capable-looking, the sort of hand that could offer support when it was needed. That was what Ben was offering her—support—but would it be right to accept? Would it be wise to come to rely on him? She was a single woman having a baby and he was a single man with no ties. They were poles apart. It was the thought that he might come to regret having offered her the hand of friendship that made her hesitate.

'Anna?' He said her name softly yet she heard the determination in his voice. He was certain that this was what he wanted to do and suddenly she didn't have the strength to resist any longer.

She placed her hand in his, refusing to think any more about the wisdom of what she was doing. She wanted to have Ben as her friend. It was as simple as that.

'Friends it is, then.'

'I know I should have told you before I accepted the job. I'm sorry.'

Anna tailed off uncertainly. It was Monday morning, a few minutes before surgery began, and she had finally screwed up enough courage to go and see Adam. He hadn't said a word while she'd told him the full story from start to finish, leaving nothing out. It had seemed the least she could do when she had told Ben everything.

She felt a little ripple run through her as she thought about Ben. He had been constantly on her mind all weekend long. She hadn't seen him yet that day and she wasn't sure how she would feel when they met again.

Was he regretting his impulsive offer of friendship, perhaps? she found herself wondering. It was easy to make a promise in the heat of the moment, but he might have had time to reconsider. She knew that she wouldn't blame him if he had, even though she would be disappointed. She liked the idea of being able to turn to him, funnily enough.

'I'm glad that you've told me now, Anna.'

She looked up when Adam spoke, feeling her stomach tighten with apprehension. 'I know I should have told you sooner...' she began, but he shook his head.

'I understand why you didn't. You were desperate to get this job. A lot of people would have done the same in your situation. Anyhow, your pregnancy doesn't pose a problem. How many weeks pregnant are you exactly?'

'Oh...um...fifteen,' she replied, feeling almost dizzy with relief. Maybe, just maybe, everything was going to work out.

'Which means that you'll be able to fulfill your contract here without putting yourself or the baby at risk in any way.' Adam flicked through his diary. 'You're with us until the end of November, by which time you'll be about thirty-two weeks by my reckoning.'

'That's right.'

He must have heard the tremulous note in her voice because he smiled reassuringly. 'There isn't a problem, Anna. Really. Now all we need to do is make sure that you have proper antenatal care. Obviously, you'll need to attend the hospital so let Eileen know when you're due to go so she can juggle your appointments around. I can see you in between visits—unless you'd prefer to register with another practice, of course. Maybe that would be best. You might feel a bit awkward consulting a colleague.'

'I'm not sure,' she murmured because she was having difficulty keeping up with what was happening.

'You don't have to decide right this very minute. Let me know when you've made up your mind and I'll make all the arrangements. Right, that's all sorted, then. Time to get ready for the morning rush.'

Adam stood up, effectively bringing the meeting to an end. Anna repeated her thanks then left the room, still feeling rather giddy about the way he had taken the news. It had gone so much better than she had dared hope that it would.

'Good morning.'

She swung round when she heard Ben's voice, seeing the concern that immediately darkened his eyes as he took stock of her expression. 'Hey, are you all right?' he said quickly.

'Fine.' She took a deep breath then smiled at him. 'Couldn't be better, in fact. I just told Adam about the baby and he was wonderful about it!'

'I told you not to worry, didn't I?' Ben said, his dark brows arching.

'I know you did but—'

'But nothing!' He started to say something else but Eileen popped her head round the office door just then to tell him that there was a phone call for him and that she was putting it through to his room.

He sighed. 'No rest for the wicked, eh? I'll catch up with you later, Anna.'

'Yes. And, Ben, thank you.' She shrugged when he glanced back. 'I appreciate you giving me that pep talk on Saturday. I wouldn't have found the nerve to tell Adam otherwise.'

'What are friends for?' he replied easily, then disappeared into his room.

Anna took a deep breath. What indeed?

CHAPTER FOUR

IT WAS another busy morning. Anna worked her way through her list of patients, only breaking off to snatch a quick cup of coffee that Eileen had brought in to her. There was such a wide variety of people to see that she found the work fascinating. She'd been specialising in renal care for the past four years so it was interesting to deal with cases that involved other areas of medicine. Harold Newcombe, a man in his early sixties, was one such case.

Anna finished testing the urine sample that Harold had brought in that day. He had non-insulin-dependent diabetes mellitus which could be treated through a combination of careful diet and weight reduction. However, Anna wasn't happy with the results of the urine test because they showed a marked increase in the level of glucose. She decided that she needed to have a word with Ben and quickly excused herself.

As luck would have it, Ben had just shown a patient out. Anna frowned as she watched Lucy Wilkins and little Sam leaving the surgery. 'Sam isn't ill again, is he?' she asked in concern.

'No, he's fine. Unfortunately, Lucy is terrified that he's going to suffer a repeat of that last incident.' Ben sighed. 'It's the third time she's brought him in to see me in the past week.'

'Oh, what a shame! The poor girl must be worried sick,' Anna said sympathetically.

'I know. I'm trying to get it across to her that the chances of Sam having another convulsion are very slim so long as she follows our advice.' He grimaced. 'If she had someone around to help her then I don't imagine she would be so uptight, but the poor kid's on her own.'

'It must be hard for her,' she said soberly, and heard him groan.

'Me and my big mouth. Sorry.'

'Don't be silly.' She realised that it might be best to change the subject so she quickly explained what she had needed to see him about. 'Mr Newcombe's glucose levels seem to be rather high so I thought you should take a look at him. Have you got time to fit him in now?'

Ben frowned as he checked his watch. 'Can you give me ten minutes? I've got a cancellation at eleven so I could see him then.'

'Fine. I was wondering if I should do a blood test as well, just to check.'

'That would be great, Anna. Thanks. Ten minutes and I'll be all yours. OK?'

She smiled, hoping that he couldn't see inside her mind at that moment. Why did the thought of Ben being 'all hers' seem so appealing?

She shrugged the thought aside as he went back into his room and she returned to her patient. Harold Newcombe looked up expectantly when she opened the door.

'Nothing wrong, is there, Nurse?'

'Your glucose level seems to be rather on the high side,' she explained, fetching the blood monitoring machine. 'Dr Cole is going to have a word with you as soon as he's free. In the meantime, I'm going to do a blood test as well.'

Harold sighed. 'I've only got myself to blame if my sugar's up. I've not been sticking to my diet as I should, I'm afraid. Doris and I went on a cruise and the food was so wonderful that I ate far more than I should have done.'

Anna laughed. 'I expect it's hard not to! I've heard how

wonderful the food is on board some of those cruise ships.'
She put the small machine on the desk. 'Was it a special
occasion?'

'Our fortieth wedding anniversary. That's why we decided to push out the boat.' Harold beamed at her, enjoying
his own joke.

Anna groaned. 'Oh, what a dreadful pun! I must remember that one. Now, all I want to do is prick your finger so
that I can get a drop of blood to test. The machine does
the rest.'

Harold nodded. 'I know. I used to sell these contraptions
once upon a time. I was a sales rep for a medical firm,' he
explained when she looked quizzically at him. 'I must have
sold hundreds of these devices over the years. I never
thought I'd be needing to use one of them, though.'

'Just view it as a test run, to see how well they work,'
she advised, smiling at him. 'Although I'm sure that people
who need to use them on a daily basis really appreciate
how easy they are. One little drop of blood and—hey,
presto—you have all the information you need.'

She quickly pricked Harold's finger then smeared the
drop of blood across a chemically coated strip and inserted
it into the machine. Within seconds she had an accurate
reading of the amount of glucose in his blood.

She glanced round when Ben tapped on the door and
came into the room. 'Perfect timing. I've just done Mr
Newcombe's blood test.'

She showed him the reading and wasn't surprised when
he frowned. 'Mr Newcombe has just come back from a
cruise,' she explained. 'Evidently, the food was excellent.'

'Which means that your diet went overboard?' Ben commented with a twinkle in his eyes.

Anna raised her eyes. 'Not another one who loves puns!'
Harold laughed. 'All men are just kids at heart, even

when you get to my age, and I could give Dr Cole a good few years! Anyway, Doctor, I know I've been a bit daft, but how bad is it?'

'The reading is certainly higher than it should have been. How have you been feeling? Have you been drinking more and wanting to pass water more frequently?'

'Yes, but I have to confess that it started before Doris and I went away,' Harold admitted.

Ben frowned. 'I see. It could be that regulating the amount and frequency of your carbohydrate intake is no longer enough and that we need to take other measures to control your diabetes.'

'Do you mean injections?' Harold asked worriedly.

'No. In cases of non-insulin-dependent diabetes, the pancreas is still producing insulin but in insufficient quantities. Sometimes careful diet is all that's needed to control it, but quite often a patient needs hypoglycaemic tablets to stimulate the pancreas to produce more insulin.'

'Oh, I see.' Harold sounded relieved. 'And you think these tablets will do the trick?'

'So long as you stick to your diet they will. However, they won't help if you over-indulge too often,' Ben warned him.

'I'm not planning on making a habit of it, not at those prices! It cost an arm and a leg, going on that cruise. It's going to be a good few years before Doris and I go on another.'

Ben laughed. 'Then there shouldn't be any problem. I'll write you out a prescription and we'll see how you get on.'

Harold stood up as Ben opened the door. 'Sounds good to me. Thanks. And thank you, love. It's been nice chatting to you. Nothing like a few minutes with a beautiful young woman to make you feel in tip-top condition, despite what all these tests might prove to the contrary!'

Anna smiled. 'I'm pleased to hear it. Anyway, I expect I'll see you again, Mr Newcombe.'

'You can be sure of it!' Harold winked at her before he left the room.

'Looks like you've made a conquest there, Nurse Clemence,' Ben observed drily. 'Careful, now. We don't want to start a rush once word gets round about you working here.'

Anna knew that he was teasing and laughed. 'And I don't think!' She sobered abruptly as a thought struck her. Ben frowned.

'What is it?' he prompted, letting the door close so no one could overhear their conversation. 'Anna?'

'I was just thinking that there won't be a problem in a few months' time.' She smiled gamely, knowing it was foolish to get upset about something so stupid. 'I can't imagine that Mr Newcombe or any other patient will be rushing to be treated by me once I'm as big as a house!'

'That's nonsense,' Ben said firmly. 'You'll be even more beautiful in a few months' time, Anna.'

He didn't say anything else before he left the room. Anna felt a little ripple run down her spine as she thought about what he had said. Had he meant it? He had sounded sincere enough but maybe he had been simply trying to cheer her up? It was what any friend would have done in the circumstances, and she'd be silly to go reading too much into it. However, it was impossible to put it out of her mind. The idea that Ben thought she was beautiful wasn't easily dismissed, oddly enough.

The day came to an end at last and Anna went up to the flat after evening surgery had finished. She changed out of her uniform and made herself something to eat then wondered how best to fill in the evening. This was the time of the day she hated most because she always felt so lonely. It was fine while she was busy working but once she had closed the door to the flat the silence seemed oppressive.

She turned on the television and watched the news. There was a game show on afterwards but she didn't feel like watching it so she switched off the television. She was just wondering if she should find something to read when she heard a noise coming from below. It sounded very much as though there was someone moving around in the surgery but she knew for a fact that everyone had left.

Anna opened the door and crept to the top of the stairs. She was just debating whether she should go down and investigate when a man walked along the hall and she gasped as she realised it was Ben.

'You scared the wits out of me,' she exclaimed as he glanced up. 'I thought we had burglars!'

'Sorry. I should have knocked and told you I was here,' he apologised. 'I didn't want to disturb you, to be honest. I thought you were probably worn out after the busy day we had.'

'I can't seem to settle,' she admitted. 'I had been planning on doing nothing more taxing than sitting in front of the television but there's nothing on that I want to watch. Anyway, what have you come back for?'

'I forgot my wallet.' Ben held up a black leather wallet then frowned. 'How would you fancy coming for a drink if you've nothing better to do? That's where I was heading when I realised that I had no cash on me.'

'Oh, I don't know…'

'Come on, Anna. It will do you good to get out for a bit and I'd be really glad of the company.'

It was hard to resist the pleading note in his voice so she didn't try. 'Why not? It will definitely beat sitting here, staring at the same four walls.'

'Great!' Ben sounded so delighted that any doubts she'd had disappeared. It was obvious that he hadn't asked her simply out of politeness, she decided, then wondered why she felt so pleased by the idea.

'I'll lock up here and meet you outside,' he continued. 'I didn't bring my car because I was going to the pub. I hope you don't mind walking. It isn't far.'

'Of course not,' she assured him, brushing aside the unsettling thought. She hurried back inside the flat, wondering if she had time to change. She sighed when it struck her that she didn't have much else to wear. Most of her clothes were getting tight now and the beige drawstring-waist trousers and loose-fitting cream cotton top she had on were the most comfortable things in her wardrobe.

In the end, she contented herself with applying a fresh coat of lipstick and running a brush through her hair. She'd unpinned it when she'd changed out of her uniform and the silky black waves fell softly around her face as she left the flat and hurried round to the front of the building where Ben was waiting for her. She couldn't help noticing the appreciative look he gave her.

'You look very nice tonight, Anna,' he said warmly. 'I love your hair loose like that.'

'Thank you,' she replied, thinking that she could easily have returned the compliment. Ben had changed out of his work clothes into slim-fitting jeans and a black V-neck sweatshirt, and she couldn't help thinking how well they suited him. She had a sudden mental picture of how he had looked in the wet running shorts and vest, and quickly drove it from her mind. Thoughts like that were best left strictly alone!

He kept up an undemanding conversation as they walked to the pub. Anna sensed that he was trying to put her at ease and appreciated his thoughtfulness. By the time they entered the pub she was ready to enjoy the unexpected outing.

'What will you have to drink?' he asked.

'Nothing alcoholic because of the baby,' she told him quickly, wondering what to choose.

'How about orange juice?' he suggested. 'They do fresh orange juice here and it's delicious.'

'That sounds lovely,' she replied immediately.

'Orange juice it is, then.' He glanced around the room then pointed to a table by the window. 'Why don't you grab a seat over there while I fetch the drinks? I won't be long.'

Anna went and sat down, smiling when Ben came back a few minutes later with their drinks. 'That was quick. Thanks.' She took a sip of the orange juice. 'It really is delicious!'

'I thought you'd enjoy it,' he said easily, pulling out a stool and sitting down. 'I come here sometimes for lunch and it's what I usually have to drink then.'

'So you come here quite a lot, do you?' she asked curiously.

'Mainly at lunchtime because it's handy for the surgery. I don't go out all that often at night.'

'You and me both!' She laughed ruefully. 'Although I'm sure you could be out every night of the week if you chose to.'

'I suppose so.' He shrugged when she looked curiously at him. 'I'm not really a party animal. I much prefer a quiet night in, to be honest.'

'Really?'

He must have heard the scepticism in her voice because he grinned. 'Yes, *really*! I did enough socialising while I was at med school to last me a lifetime.'

'Thank heavens for that! I was beginning to think there

was something wrong with you. I know the reputation you doctors have for enjoying yourselves,' she teased.

'Probably well founded in a lot of cases.'

'But not in your case?'

He shrugged. 'As I say, I did my share of partying when I was younger. I simply outgrew that stage.'

'I see.' Anna had a feeling that there was a lot that he wasn't telling her. However, she decided that it would be more tactful not to question him further. If Ben had wanted her to know more about his life then he would have told her, she reasoned.

'So how do you spend your free time if you don't go in for wild parties?' she asked instead.

'I don't seem to have had all that much free time recently,' he replied noncommittally.

Anna frowned. 'But you must do something. I know that you go running so is that your main form of relaxation?'

'I suppose so. How about you? What sort of hobbies do you enjoy, Anna?'

He neatly steered the conversation away from himself but Anna had to admit that she was intrigued about why he seemed so loath to talk about himself. 'Oh, reading, cinema, going to the theatre, nothing too taxing. I'm certainly not into sport!'

He laughed at that. 'I can't say that I actually enjoy it. It's a necessary evil, shall we say. I spend so much of my life sitting in a chair that I feel I should make the effort to get some exercise.'

'You seemed fairly dedicated to me,' she countered. 'Not many people would have gone running in that rain.'

'That was by accident rather than design, I assure you. I had planned on being safely back home before the rain started. Unfortunately, that storm caught me by surprise.'

'You and me both,' she admitted ruefully. 'I couldn't believe it when the heavens opened like that.'

'Maybe it was a good thing that it happened.' He shrugged when she looked at him blankly. 'I don't imagine we would be sitting here now, sharing a friendly drink, if it hadn't.'

She grimaced. 'No, I expect you're right.'

'They say that every cloud has a silver lining,' he said with a completely straight face.

'Not again!' she groaned. 'You and Harold Newcombe should form your own society.'

'Punners Anonymous,' he suggested with his tongue very firmly in his cheek.

Anna burst out laughing. 'You're incorrigible!'

'Maybe I am, but it's good to see you laughing like that, Anna. I get the impression that there haven't been all that many occasions when you could enjoy yourself recently.'

She sighed softly. 'You're right, of course. It's been one problem after another for weeks now. I keep waiting for the other shoe to drop and something else to go wrong.'

'Nothing is going to go wrong,' he said firmly. 'All you need to do now is concentrate on the baby.'

'I suppose so.' She laid her hand protectively across her stomach and was surprised by the expression of tenderness in his eyes when she glanced up. She cleared her throat, not wanting him to see how touched she was. 'As long as the baby is healthy, that's my main concern.'

'Do you mind what it is?' he asked quietly, picking up his glass.

'No. As long as it's fit and healthy, I really don't care,' she replied truthfully.

'When are you due for a scan? It's usually done around sixteen weeks, isn't it? Maybe they will be able to tell you then if it's a boy or a girl.'

'I've an appointment for next Wednesday, although I'm not sure if I want to know what sex the baby is.' She grimaced as a thought struck her. 'I wonder what Eileen will say when I tell her why I need the time off?'

'I don't imagine that she will say anything.' He shook his head reprovingly. 'You must stop worrying about what people are going to think. You haven't done anything wrong, Anna.'

'I know, but—'

'But me no buts, as I believe someone once said, only don't ask me who,' he declared, finishing his drink. 'Fancy another?' he began, then broke off when his mobile phone rang. 'Excuse me a moment.'

He made his way to the door so that he could hear what the caller was saying. Anna finished her orange juice then looked up as he came back. She felt her heart skip a beat when she saw the grim expression on his face.

'Is there something wrong?' she asked worriedly.

'I'm afraid that I'll have to go.' He stepped back as she immediately rose to her feet. 'I'm really sorry about this, Anna. I hate to have to run out on you like this.'

'Don't worry about it,' she assured him, although she couldn't help wondering what had happened.

'I'll walk you back to the surgery,' he told her as they left the pub. He shook his head when she started to protest. 'I insist. It's dark and I prefer to know that you've got home safely.'

His consideration warmed her even though it didn't explain what was so urgent that he had needed to cut short the evening. Anna sighed as she realised that it was none of her business. The phone call could have been from anyone—a friend, a relative, a girlfriend even.

She felt a little wave of sickness wash through her at the thought. She couldn't believe that it had never occurred to her before that Ben might have a girlfriend. After all, he was an extremely attractive man so it would have been strange if he *hadn't* had one!

Fortunately, Ben didn't say very much as they walked back to the surgery. He seemed rather abstracted, in fact. Anna was glad because she didn't think that she could have kept up a conversation right then. The thought of him hurrying off to meet another woman after he had left her made her feel all churned up inside. She didn't like to think about him with another woman, funnily enough. She didn't like it one little bit.

She went into the flat after he had gone and switched on the sitting-room lights then went into each room in turn, switching on lights, not wanting to sit there on her own in the darkness. Yet no matter how bright the lights were or how loud the volume on the television was, nothing could take away the feeling of loneliness. She missed Ben's company. She missed *him*. But why?

She had no claim on Ben. He was just someone she worked with, a colleague who had been kind and supportive. Nevertheless, she couldn't deny that there was an ache in her heart now that he had left, a feeling inside her that something important was suddenly missing from her life.

She got up abruptly to draw the curtains, not wanting to go any further down that route. Wherever Ben was, she doubted whether he was missing her!

'Dr Knight explained that you would need some time off. Wednesday won't be a problem, dear. I can juggle your appointments around to make sure that you finish on time.'

Anna smiled her thanks although she was well aware of the curiosity in the receptionist's eyes. Eileen was obviously wondering why she needed the time off but she still hadn't made up her mind what she was going to tell her.

An edited version of the truth seemed best but she had never been good at lying.

That thought immediately reminded her of what Ben had said to her a few days earlier and she bit back a sigh. *Everything* seemed to remind her of Ben! He was occupying far too much of her thoughts at the moment but she wasn't sure what to do about it. She couldn't ignore him when they worked together, nor should she have to. Ben was her friend so why should she feel that she had to ignore him?

'Thanks, Eileen. If there's any problem then I could work a bit later on Tuesday if it would help. I don't mind giving up my lunch-break if anyone needs to see me urgently,' she offered, quickly returning her mind to the most pressing problem.

'I can't see why you should have to do that,' Eileen replied firmly. 'You do more than enough as it is. Wouldn't you agree, Ben?'

Anna felt her pulse leap as she saw Ben coming out of the office with his post. She busied herself straightening the display of leaflets on the end of the counter as he came to join them. She hadn't spoken to him as yet that morning and she wanted to be sure that there was no trace of anything in her voice when she did. Letting Ben know what a miserable night she'd spent after he'd left her was out of the question.

Eileen quickly explained what they had been discussing and he frowned. 'Certainly not. There's no reason why you should feel that you have to make up any time, Anna.'

'It was just a thought,' she said huskily, avoiding his eyes. 'Thanks again, Eileen. I appreciate it.'

She quickly left the waiting room and hurried back to her room, pausing when she heard footsteps behind her.

She felt herself colour when she saw that Ben had followed her.

'Are you feeling all right this morning, Anna?' He studied her closely, a trace of concern in his eyes. 'You looked a bit upset when you went rushing off just now.'

'Did I? I've no idea why, except that it was a bit of drag having to force myself out of bed this morning. I stayed up to watch the late night film last night,' she explained, hoping to distract him from asking any more awkward questions. How would he feel if she explained that her tiredness was due to the fact that she had lain awake thinking about him? 'And I'm paying for it this morning!'

'Serves you right!' he declared. 'You should take a leaf out of my book. I was in bed with the lights out by ten-thirty.'

But had he been on his own? she found herself wondering, then had to bite her tongue to stop herself asking a question like that.

'Did I say something?' he asked, frowning. He touched her hand, his frown deepening when she quickly withdrew it. 'Anna, what's the matter?'

'Nothing that a good night's sleep won't cure,' she replied lightly, although the thought of some unknown woman sharing his bed was like a dagger through her heart. She fixed a smile to her mouth, terrified that he would guess what was going through her head at that moment. 'Extra brownie points for you, though, for having an early night.'

'I deserve them, too, for being so good.' He smiled but his gaze was oddly intent, as though he suspected that she wasn't telling him the whole truth. It was a struggle to meet his eyes but Anna was desperate not to arouse his suspicions any further.

'Anyway, I enjoyed last night, Anna. We must do it again some time, if you'd like to.'

Anna smiled and nodded but she was relieved when he went into his room without saying anything else. There wasn't going to be a repeat of last night. She had made up her mind about that. What point was there in letting herself dream about something that was never going to happen?

'Just good friends' was such a cliché, but in this instance that was exactly what it had to mean.

CHAPTER FIVE

THE time flew by and another week passed. Anna was due at the hospital on the Wednesday afternoon for a scan. She worked her way through her morning list then went up to the flat and changed. Her appointment was for two o'clock so she needed to catch the bus before one if she wanted to be on time. However, she had to admit to feeling a bit nervous about what was going to happen that afternoon.

Ultrasound scans were used to confirm the size of a foetus and its expected delivery date. They could also show any abnormalities, like spina bifida or anencephaly, for instance. She couldn't help worrying whether everything would be all right.

She left the flat a short time later and walked to the bus stop, groaning when it suddenly started to rain again. She was just struggling to put up her umbrella when Ben drew up in his car.

'Want a lift?' he offered, leaning over to open the door for her.

Anna shook her head. She had been careful to limit the amount of time she spent around him since that evening they had gone to the pub together, and it didn't seem wise to accept. 'No, it's fine, really. Anyway, I'm going to the hospital and I don't want to take you out of your way.'

'I'm going that way, as it happens, so hop in.'

There was no way that she could refuse without making a fuss. She reluctantly folded her umbrella and got into the car. 'Thanks. Are you going to visit someone in hospital, then?'

'No, I'm going to spend a couple of hours going around the estate agents in the area.' He checked his rear-view mirror then pulled away from the kerb.

'Oh, I see. Does that mean that you're looking for somewhere to live?' she asked in surprise.

'Uh-huh.' Ben was concentrating on the traffic and he waited until he had overtaken a slow-moving lorry before continuing. 'I've been renting a flat up till now, but the owners are due back at the end of the month so I'll have to find somewhere else to live.'

'Not easy,' she observed sympathetically. 'The price of rented accommodation in Winton is horrendous.'

'Actually, I'm hoping to buy a place this time rather than renting.' He shrugged. 'It's about time I put down some roots and now seems like the right moment to do it seeing as Adam has given me a permanent contract.'

'I didn't know you weren't permanently employed at the surgery,' she exclaimed in surprise.

'I came here originally as a locum,' he explained. 'However, I've really enjoyed working here so when Adam suggested that I stay on, I jumped at the chance.'

Anna frowned as she thought about what he had said. She couldn't help wondering why he hadn't taken a permanent position before. He must have had other offers because he was an excellent doctor, but obviously he had chosen to do locum work instead. She was on the point of questioning him further when he continued.

'The one drawback about living in Winton is the cost of property here. With the town being so convenient for people working in Manchester, property fetches premium prices. I thought I'd found myself a bargain a couple of weeks ago but I was gazumped.'

'You mean that someone put in a better offer for the house you wanted to buy?' she asked.

'Ten thousand pounds better, would you believe? Remember that phone call I had when we were out for a drink?' He smiled wryly when she nodded. 'It was the vendor of the house I was after, asking me if I was prepared to match the new offer he'd had. Fat chance of me being able to come up with that kind of money!'

'Oh, I see!' she exclaimed. 'I thought it…' She stopped as she realised what she had been about to say, that she'd thought it had been his girlfriend calling him. She damped down the rush of relief she felt when she saw him look at her.

'I thought it must have been something important when you rushed off like that,' she fibbed, rather than admitting the truth. However, she couldn't deny that her heart felt all the lighter for knowing who had been phoning him that night.

'And you were right. I went straight round to the house to see if I could persuade him to stick to our deal.' He shook his head when she looked at him. 'It didn't work, I'm afraid.'

'Hence today's trip into the city?'

'Exactly. I've tried all the estate agents in Winton but everything on their books is way beyond my price range. I've decided that I shall have to look further afield.'

'But not too far to make travelling into work each day a problem,' she put in quickly.

'That's the tricky bit, of course. Still, enough of my woes. I bet you're really excited about this scan.'

Anna sighed. 'I think nervous is a better way to describe how I feel.'

'Why on earth are you nervous?' he began, then frowned. 'You're worried in case the scan shows something is wrong—is that it, Anna?'

'Yes. I don't think I could bear it if there were any problems at this stage,' she admitted huskily, unable to keep the tremor out of her voice.

'The chances of there being anything wrong with your baby are very slim, Anna,' he said gently. 'You must know that.'

'I do. Well, the *logical* bit of me does. The other bit of me can't help worrying.'

He sighed heavily. 'I can understand that. This baby is just so special, isn't it? But I'm sure everything will be fine.'

She summoned a smile, appreciating the fact that he was trying his best to reassure her. 'I'm sure it will.'

'Of course it will.' He changed the subject then, chatting away about the type of house he was looking for. Anna knew that he was trying to take her mind off what was going to happen that afternoon and appreciated his thoughtfulness.

She realised all of a sudden how much better she felt, having him there with her. It hadn't occurred to her before how much of an ordeal this visit to the hospital was, but it didn't seem nearly so stressful with Ben there.

He stopped the car in front of the entrance to the antenatal clinic then turned to her. 'What time do you think you'll be finished here?'

'I don't know. Hopefully it shouldn't take more than an hour or so, but it's hard to say for certain,' she explained. 'Why?'

'Because I'll give you a lift home, of course.' He shook his head when she started to protest. 'Don't be silly, Anna. What's the point in you taking the bus when I can give you a lift? I'll come back later for you. In about an hour's time. OK?'

'OK.' Anna got out of the car, sighing as she watched him driving away. One day some lucky woman was going to realise just how fortunate she was to have Ben taking care of her. She couldn't help feeling a bit jealous at the thought. How wonderful life would be if she had someone like him around to share all the bad times as well as the good.

Her mind took a small sideways step before she could stop it. How wonderful it would be to have *Ben* around!

In the event, Anna was still waiting to be go through for her scan when Ben came back. The antenatal clinic had been packed that day and she'd had to wait her turn while various tests were done. He sat down beside her, grinning when he saw the queues of women in various stages of pregnancy walking about.

'Who said that the birth-rate figures are dropping? They obviously haven't visited their local antenatal clinic recently!'

Anna laughed at the wry note in his voice although she couldn't help feeling rather guilty at the thought of him having to wait around. 'There do seem to be a lot of expectant mums here today. Look, Ben, I understand if you want to get off home. I don't expect you to wait for me.'

'Don't be silly. I'm not letting you trail all the way back to Winton on the bus.'

She sighed because she could tell that it would be a waste of time arguing with him. It seemed a bit rich that he should be spending his free afternoon sitting in a hospital, though.

'Actually, what I've been meaning to ask you was why you had decided to come here for your antenatal care. Surely you should be attending the clinic where you were treated?' he said curiously.

'It's simply a matter of convenience,' she explained. 'I realised when I took the job at the surgery that I would have problems getting to the clinic. It's miles away and, without a car, it would take me hours to get there and back on the bus.'

'I see.' He frowned heavily. 'If you ever feel that you want to change your mind, just tell me, Anna. I'd be glad to give you a lift any time you need it.'

'That's very kind of you but I'm quite happy coming here,' she told him truthfully. 'The clinic has passed on my notes so the doctors here know all about my case history.'

'And there were no problems today?'

'Problems?' she queried, then realised that he was alluding to her first visit to the hospital when she had been met with a less then sympathetic reaction by one of the nurses. It warmed her heart to know that he had remembered what she had told him and she smiled. 'No, it's been fine. Everyone's been lovely.'

'Good. But the offer's there if you ever need it,' he replied firmly.

It was another ten minutes before the nurse called her name. Anna got up, pausing when the nurse glanced at Ben. 'You can come as well if you like,' she told him.

'Oh, but…' Anna began, but the nurse had already hurried away.

Ben stood up. 'Would you like me to come with you, Anna?'

She hesitated but the offer was far too tempting to refuse. Now that the time had actually arrived when she would have the scan, she was a bundle of nerves. 'Would you mind? I know it's silly but it would be nice to have someone with me.'

'Of course I don't mind!' Ben declared in exasperation. 'I can't wait to get a look at this little fellow.'

Anna laughed. 'This little fellow could be a little girl for all we know.'

'Who cares? It still would be nice to have a peek at him or her.'

She smiled when she heard the excitement in his voice. Maybe he had made the offer because he had sensed how apprehensive she was, but he seemed to be genuinely *interested* in seeing the baby. After all the heartache of recent weeks it was a wonderful feeling to know that he cared. All of a sudden she knew that she was looking forward to it herself. With Ben there beside her there didn't seem any reason to be afraid.

'Then what are we waiting for?' she said lightly, closing her mind to the small voice that was whispering a warning. She didn't need any warnings because she had no intention of letting herself get carried away. She wasn't going to fall into the trap of hoping that he would be around for ever.

She glanced round as he took her arm, felt her heart give an oddly painful lurch. She was going to miss not having Ben there in the future to turn to.

'There's the baby's head…and that's an arm.'

Anna gasped as she stared at the monitor. 'It's so tiny!'

'It will soon grow.' The operator laughed as she moved the transducer—the part of the machine that emitted the ultrasound waves—across Anna's abdomen. 'You'll notice a huge difference next time you come. At the moment you could be looking at any little moving blob unless you know what you're seeing. But give it a few more weeks and you'll be able to see the baby perfectly and tell what sex it is. I'm afraid that it's moving about too much today for me to tell if it's a boy or a girl.'

'I'm not sure if I want to know,' she declared. 'I think I'd rather it was a surprise.'

'Sure you wouldn't like advance warning so you'll know what colour to paint the nursery?' Ben teased.

'I'll play it safe and opt for something neutral,' she retorted.

'Isn't that the father's job?' The operator put in, looking pointedly at him.

Anna flushed when she realised that the woman thought that Ben was the baby's father. It was an understandable mistake, but she knew that she should set her straight. However, before she could say anything Ben laughed.

'It's a fair trade, really. I expect most men are more than happy to swop a bit of decorating for all the pain and strain that goes with having a baby.'

The young woman chuckled. 'Too right they are! If men had to bear the children, the world's population would have died out centuries ago.'

She leant over and briskly wiped away the gel she had squeezed onto Anna's tummy to enable the transducer to move more smoothly over her skin. 'That's it, then. Would you like a picture for the family album?'

'Oh, yes, please,' Anna agreed at once, reaching for her bag.

'Here, let me get that.' Ben quickly paid for the photograph then helped her down from the couch.

'I must pay you for that,' she began as they left the room, but he shook his head.

'Don't be silly.' His smile was warm as he looked at the photograph. 'It's amazing. Even when you know all about how babies develop, it's still fantastic to think that little blob will one day turn into a real, live human being.'

'It is. I only wish...' She stopped.

'That Jo could have been here to see it,' he finished for her with a wealth of compassion in his voice.

'Yes.' It was an effort to smile when she felt her eyes welling with tears. 'She would have been so thrilled to see that picture.'

'I know it must be hard, Anna.' He took her hand and held it as they left the clinic. 'You just have to hang onto the thought that your sister would have been so proud of what you're doing.'

'I'll try,' she agreed softly.

She took a deep breath then deliberately withdrew her hand, knowing that it would be foolish to get too used to having him support her like that. Even though she had appreciated Ben's help that day, she mustn't let herself rely too heavily on him. Once her job at the surgery came to an end she doubted if she would see very much of him. Ben had his own life to lead and she'd have hers. It was an oddly painful thought.

The following day was fairly quiet for once, but they made up for it on Friday. The phone never stopped ringing all morning long so that even Eileen was frazzled by the time lunchtime arrived. Both Adam and Ben were needed to complete all the house calls after morning surgery ended.

It turned out that an outbreak of food poisoning was to blame for all the people who were suffering from sickness and diarrhoea. They'd been guests at a wedding reception held in the church hall the previous day. Once Adam had discovered that, he contacted the medical officer at the environmental health department and they immediately agreed to investigate the cause of the problem. By the time Friday came to an end everyone was worn out.

'Am I glad today is over!' Ben declared as he came into the office. 'That has to be one of the worst days I've ever had.'

'Do you think it's wise to tempt fate?' Anna retorted. 'There's still Saturday morning to go. It's your turn to take surgery this week, isn't it?'

'Don't remind me. With my luck we'll probably have

another outbreak of something dreadful.' He groaned at the thought then moved out of the way as Eileen bustled in to collect her coat.

'What a day!' the receptionist said. 'I'm certainly not sorry to see the back of it. Still, Dr Knight told me that the new receptionist is starting on Monday so that should make my life a bit easier.'

'Not before time either,' Ben declared. 'You do sterling work, Eileen. I don't know how you kept up with all the calls today.'

'Oh, I just try to do my bit,' Eileen replied cheerfully. 'Anyway, I'd better be off. Ron and I are going to our daughter's tonight to babysit. She's a community midwife,' she explained for Anna's benefit, 'so she doesn't get that many evenings free, and I don't want to be late.'

She had just left when Adam appeared. 'I've just had a fax from the health department to say that they suspect the source of the food poisoning was the chicken that was served at the evening buffet. It probably wasn't cooked thoroughly.'

'What a shame!' Anna said. 'Who did the catering for the reception?'

'I'm not sure. It wasn't a firm from Winton, though.' He sighed. 'Evidently, the reception had been booked at the Willows Hotel but they'd had to change the venue after the accident.'

'What accident was that?' she asked curiously.

'They had a gas explosion there a couple of months ago,' Ben explained. 'I'm surprised you didn't hear about it because it was in all the papers. It completely demolished the new wing and the hotel has been closed ever since.'

'Which is why the Reynolds had to hold their wedding reception in the church hall,' Adam put in. 'Anyway, I'll love you and leave you, as they say. Will you lock up and set the alarm, Ben?'

'Sure.' Ben laughed as Adam left the office. 'There'll be no excuse to forget that wedding anniversary!'

'There certainly won't, although I'm sure the bride and groom would have preferred a less memorable end to their big day!' She followed him into the corridor. 'That's it, then. I'll see you on Monday.'

'Before you go, Anna, how do you fancy coming house-hunting with me over the weekend? I've been meaning to ask you all day but haven't had the chance. I got some leaflets from the estate agents yesterday and there's a couple of places which look promising.'

'When were you thinking of going?' she asked hesitantly, wondering if it would be wise to go with him. The more time that she spent with him, the harder it would be to say goodbye when the time came, she reasoned.

'Saturday afternoon or Sunday. I don't mind really. Whichever is most convenient for you.'

'Are you sure you want me to tag along?' She sighed when she saw his eyebrows rise. 'You're not just being kind, are you? Trying to save me from spending the week-end on my own?'

'You consider being dragged around a lot of dire houses as being *kind*?' He shook his head. 'The pressure of work is obviously getting to you, Nurse Clemence.'

She chuckled. 'How do you know they are going to be dire? They could be little palaces.'

'Not in the price range that I can afford,' he replied cheerfully. 'So if you think it's going to be wall-to-wall luxury, forget it. That's one of the reasons why I want you to come, actually. I'm not bad at the practical work—painting, decorating, the odd bit of woodwork—but I'm useless at visualising how a place will look. I need your visionary eye to bring out the potential in the properties we see.'

'Really? I didn't realise I was so talented,' she retorted, then laughed when he pulled a face. She knew that she should refuse but suddenly the thought of not having to spend the whole weekend on her own was too tempting to resist. 'All right, then, I'd love to come.'

'Brilliant! Let's make it Sunday around ten? Is that OK?'

'Fine,' she agreed.

She left him to finish locking up and went up to the flat, and for once the evening didn't seem to drag as it usually did. It made a big difference, having something to look forward to.

She sighed because there was no way that she could ignore the truth. It made a big difference, having an outing with *Ben* to look forward to. Maybe it was a mistake and maybe she would regret it, but she couldn't deny that she enjoyed being with him.

Sunday dawned bright and clear for once. Anna was up before eight and took a shower. She washed and blow-dried her hair, taking extra care to make sure that it fell smoothly around her face. Choosing what to wear was a problem because even in a couple of weeks her waistline had expanded quite considerably. She tried on her jeans, but there was no way that she could fasten the top button and even doing up the zip was uncomfortable.

In the end she was forced to wear the beige trousers again, teamed with a pale aqua silk shirt which had been an impulse buy in the sales the previous year. The fine material clung to her body rather more than she would have liked, outlining the fullness of her breasts and the curve of her tummy, but it was the prettiest thing she had to wear. Anyway, Ben knew that she was pregnant so it wasn't as though she had to hide the fact. It was just that she didn't want him to think that she looked unattractive. She sighed when she realised how silly that thought was in the circumstances.

He arrived right on time, grinning when he saw her coming down the steps. 'Great. I'm glad you're ready. We can get straight off. We have a lot to do.'

Anna slid into the passenger seat and fastened her seat belt. 'That sounds ominous. How many properties are there to view?'

'If I tell you that, you might change your mind,' he responded, turning the car around. 'Let's just say enough to keep us busy and leave it at that.'

Three hours later Anna knew that he'd been wise not to say too much. They had seen seven houses by that point, although only in the very loosest sense of the word. Most had been so awful that they had done no more than drive past; it hadn't been worth stopping to look inside when the exteriors had been so offputting.

Ben pulled to the side of the road and rescued the inch-thick wedge of advertising leaflets from the back seat. 'Whoever writes these should be shot. Listen to this. ''Highly desirable residence with wonderful views over the surrounding countryside'',' he quoted. 'Maybe if you stood on the roof with a pair of binoculars.'

'Which one was that?' Anna asked, leaning over to look at the leaflet. 'Oh, not that dreadful little hovel surrounded by all those high-rise flats!'

'That's the one. Is it us or is it them, do you think? They obviously think that bijou residence is worth a lot of money, whereas *I'd* expect to be *paid* for living there!'

Anna sighed when she heard the dejection in his voice. 'There must be something else. Let me have a look.' She flicked through the leaflets then paused when she came to one near the bottom of the pile. 'How about this one?'

Ben frowned as he skimmed through the details. 'It says that it needs some work doing to it, which probably means that it's falling to bits.'

'It can't be any worse than what we've seen. Come on. Let's give it a shot. What have we got to lose?' she said encouragingly.

'Nothing, I suppose.' He suddenly leant over, obviously intending to kiss her cheek. It was pure coincidence that she happened to turn at that moment so that his mouth brushed hers instead.

Anna felt her heart tumble around inside her as she felt the gentle pressure of his lips. They felt so warm and tasted so sweet that she made no attempt to avoid the contact. There was a moment when the pressure seemed to increase ever so slightly before he abruptly drew back. Anna took a quick breath but it did little to quell the hot shivers that were racing through her body.

'Thanks for coming today, Anna. Not many people would give up their Sunday off to come trailing around like this,' he said, starting the engine.

'My pleasure.' It was an effort to respond naturally when she heard the grating note in his voice. She shot him a wary glance as he put the car into gear, wondering what had caused it.

Was Ben disturbed by that kiss, as she was? Or was he simply embarrassed because he had never meant it to happen like that? He had intended to bestow a token kiss on her cheek as a measure of his thanks and had found himself in the awkward position of kissing her properly.

Her heart ached as she realised that was the most likely explanation. She knew it was foolish to feel so disappointed but she couldn't help it. All of a sudden she found herself wishing that she had met Ben at a different stage in her life. Things might have turned out very differently then.

Lilac Cottage was situated at the end of a narrow lane that was overgrown on both sides with bushes. Ben stopped the car in front of the house and sat for a moment, staring through the windscreen.

'It's better than I thought it would be,' he admitted slowly. 'And the view from the back garden must be spectacular.'

'Shall we go and knock?' Anna suggested, not deaf to the thread of excitement in his voice.

'Why not?' He got out of the car, waiting for her to join him so that they could walk up the path together. There was little doubt that the cottage would need a great deal of work, but she had a good feeling about the place.

They knocked on the door but there was no reply. Ben sighed when a second attempt didn't gain any better results. 'Doesn't look as though there's anyone home. We'll have to come back another day.'

'Maybe we could sneak a look round the back while we're here,' she suggested, loath to leave it at that. She tried the gate at the side of the cottage and grinned at him when she discovered that it wasn't locked. 'Seems our luck's in.'

'I suppose it won't hurt to have a quick look,' he conceded. 'I'll blame you if the owners come back and kick up a fuss.'

'Oh, my hero!' she taunted. She pushed open the gate then gave a gasp of delight. 'It's beautiful! Just have a look, Ben.'

He put his hands on her shoulders and edged her aside so that he could see. 'Isn't it just? Wow what a view!'

He was obviously completely overwhelmed by the wonderful view over the rolling Cheshire countryside and seemed oblivious to the fact that he still had hold of her. Anna wasn't, however. Her senses had been heightened already by that accidental kiss and now they seemed to run riot all of a sudden. She could feel her heart starting to beat in short, jerky bursts, as though she were suffering from an attack of cardiac hiccups.

She closed her eyes, praying that she wouldn't do anything to give herself away. She couldn't bear to embarrass him or herself by letting him know how she felt. However, the moment she heard the concern in his voice she knew that her prayers had gone unanswered.

'Anna, what is it? Are you feeling all right?'

'I…um…I'm fine,' she murmured, but Ben obviously wasn't convinced. He turned her to face him and his expression was stern.

'Tell me what's wrong. If you don't feel well, say so. It's probably my fault for dragging you all round the county like this.'

'I'm fine,' she repeated, although she could feel the guilty colour washing up her face. She was far from fine and she hated having to lie to him, but she had no choice.

'Oh, Anna.'

She felt a tingle run down her spine when she heard that grating note in his voice once again. Her breath caught sharply when she saw the way he was looking at her. When he bent towards her she couldn't have moved to save her life because she was so shocked. Ben was looking at her as though he found her deeply attractive, but that couldn't be right!

His mouth was so gentle at first as it covered hers. Anna had a feeling that he was half expecting her to object but not a single word escaped her lips. She was too stunned to object, too shocked to feel anything other than pleasure when he drew her closer and kissed her with a new-found confidence and assurance that made her head spin so that she felt giddy and breathless all at the same time.

She wrapped her arms around his neck to steady herself but, no matter how dizzy she felt, she knew that she didn't want him to stop what he was doing. She wanted him to kiss her again and again, to keep on kissing her and never, ever stop. When Ben kissed her like this, it felt as though anything was possible!

He dragged his mouth away from hers at last but only so that he could scatter a shower of kisses over her face. Anna murmured softly when she felt his lips touching her eyelids and cheekbones, the tip of her nose. It felt as though she were being sprinkled with fairy dust because the kisses were so delicate, yet despite how light they were each and every one left behind a tiny pinpoint of warmth on her skin.

She shivered convulsively and felt his arms tighten as he drew her closer, felt his lips begin a tantalising return journey. Her own lips parted on a soft sigh of anticipation as she waited…

'Hello! Are you still there? Can you hear me?'

Anna jumped as a woman's voice came floating towards them. She just had a moment to try and gather her wits before Ben let her go as an elderly lady appeared from the front of the house.

'Oh, good, you haven't left. I was upstairs when you knocked and I'm afraid it takes me ages to get down the stairs nowadays.'

Ben summoned a smile but Anna could tell that it was an effort for him to behave naturally. 'We didn't think there was anyone at home,' he explained politely. 'I really must apologise for being so rude as to take a look in the back garden.'

'That doesn't matter, dear. Come along in and I'll show you around the house. I'm Agnes Williams, by the way.'

Ben quickly completed the introductions then waited for the old lady to lead the way. He caught hold of Anna's arm as she went to follow and she couldn't help noticing the troubled light in his eyes as he turned her to face him.

'About what happened just now, Anna, well, I'm sorry. I don't know what came over me but it won't happen again, I promise you that.'

'Forget it.' Somehow she managed to smile but inside it felt as though her heart were weeping. The fact that Ben believed that he needed to apologise for kissing her was a good indication of how he felt. Had it been a momentary aberration on his behalf, something to regret? Probably. However, she knew that it wasn't an excuse she could use.

She took a deep breath before she followed the old lady into the cottage. Maybe it would be best to heed her own advice and forget what had happened, but it would be hard to do that. She couldn't pretend, neither could she lie to herself. It hadn't been a temporary lapse on her part. She had known exactly what she was doing and had wanted Ben to kiss her more than she had wanted anything in the whole of her life.

It was going to be impossible to forget that.

CHAPTER SIX

'It's just perfect, exactly what I've been looking for.'

Anna smiled when she heard the excitement in Ben's voice. It was obvious that he was completely taken with the cottage, not that she blamed him.

She sighed as she turned to look out of the bedroom window. She couldn't help thinking longingly how much she would love to live in a place like this. There was a lot of work that needed to be done, of course, but the cottage would respond wonderfully to a bit of TLC.

'So, what do you think?' Ben came and stood beside her as Agnes murmured something about making them a cup of tea and tactfully left the room.

'I think it's beautiful,' she said sincerely, avoiding his eyes by keeping her gaze focused on the view. She was still having a hard time coming to terms with what had happened earlier so it seemed wiser.

'It is.' Ben frowned as he looked around the bedroom with its sloping eaves and uneven wooden floor. 'It looks *lived in*, a real home rather than a showplace. I know that I could have every modern convenience known to man if I bought a house on that new estate that's being built on the outskirts of Winton, but—'

'It wouldn't be a patch on this place,' she cut in.

'No, it wouldn't,' he agreed, grinning at her.

'Then what are you waiting for? Why don't you make Mrs Williams an offer?' She saw him hesitate and knew what he was thinking. 'I know it's going to take a lot of hard work to bring this place up to scratch, Ben, but it would be worth it, wouldn't it?'

'It would. You've talked me into it, not that I needed much persuading, mind you!'

He laughed as he led the way from the bedroom. Anna sighed as she took a last look around. There was no point wishing that she could afford a place like this because there was no chance of that happening.

Agnes had the tea made when they went downstairs. 'Sit yourselves down, both of you.' She filled the cups then looked expectantly at them. 'So what's the verdict? I got the impression that you liked the cottage.'

'We do,' Ben replied truthfully. 'I want to make you an offer, in fact.'

'Oh, good!' Agnes beamed with delight. 'I was hoping that you would. This house needs a family living in it again to bring it back to life.'

She looked pointedly at Anna, who flushed. It was obvious that the old lady had guessed that she was pregnant and she wasn't sure if she should explain that Ben wasn't the baby's father.

She glanced at him for guidance but he merely shrugged. Was he hoping that it would help persuade Agnes to accept his offer if she believed that he was buying the cottage to raise his family there? she wondered.

She couldn't help feeling a little hurt at the thought that he might be using her to his own ends, although she didn't say anything. She sipped her tea, listening while the old lady chattered on about the cottage and the time she had spent there.

'I've always loved living here,' Agnes explained. 'But it's been very lonely since my Cyril died last year. My sons both live down south so they don't get much chance to visit very often. That's why I decided to sell up and move to a retirement home. At least I'll have some company there.'

'Have you had many offers for the cottage?' Ben asked, putting down his cup.

'A few, but most have seemed more interested in buying the place so that they can pull it down.' Agnes sounded indignant. 'One man in particular is dying to get his hands on it, but he let it slip that he intends to knock the place down and build two luxury houses here instead. There's no way that I want that happening!'

'Well, I certainly won't be wanting to knock the cottage down,' Ben assured her. 'I plan on living here for a long time to come.'

Anna sighed when she saw Agnes looking at her again. 'It would be nice to know that there were children playing in the garden again,' the old lady commented happily.

'Hopefully, there will be one day, but I'm not sure when it's going to happen,' Ben told her gently. 'Anna is just a friend who very kindly offered to come with me today.'

'Oh, I see. I thought…' Agnes broke off, looking embarrassed. 'Well, never mind. So long as I know that you aren't planning on knocking down the cottage, I'll be happy to accept your offer.'

'You have my word on it,' he replied sincerely.

Anna sipped her tea. She had to confess that she was relieved that Ben had told the old lady the truth. She should have known that he would, of course. He was too innately honest to lie.

That thought was less comforting than it should have been because she couldn't help thinking about what he had said to her after that kiss. He had told the truth then—that he was sorry for having let it happen, and it hurt to know that he regretted it. It was an effort to respond naturally as they drove back to Winton a short time later but Anna knew that she had to put the events of the day behind her, hard though it was going to be.

'How about going out to celebrate?' Ben drew up in the surgery car park and turned to her.

'Celebrate?' she repeated uncertainly.

'The fact that I've found the perfect place to live, of course.' He sighed theatrically. 'I think it's a reason for celebrating even if you don't!'

She summoned a smile but it was hard to respond with enthusiasm when her heart felt so heavy. 'Of course it's wonderful that you've found a place you like so much...'

'But? Come on, out with it.' He folded his arms and stared at her. 'Why do I get the distinct impression that you have reservations?'

'I don't. Not about the cottage, anyway,' she assured him honestly. However, she had serious reservations about what he had suggested. Would it really be wise to spend any more time with him that day when her thoughts were in such turmoil? she found herself wondering.

'I'm just feeling a bit tired, that's all,' she explained carefully. 'I think I'd rather stay in and have a quiet evening in front of the television.'

'I should have thought of that. I'm sorry, Anna. I didn't mean to tire you out today.'

His tone was so contrite that she was stricken with remorse for the small white lie. Ben had offered to be her friend and it wasn't his fault if he was sticking to their arrangement.

'I know you didn't,' she said huskily.

'It is only tiredness? You're sure you feel all right apart from that?' he asked in obvious concern.

'I'm sure.' She quickly opened the car door, wanting to get away before she did something foolish. How would he feel if she told him that the real reason she didn't want to

spend any more time with him that day was because she
didn't trust herself? Would he be shocked if she admitted
that she wanted him to put his arms around her again and
kiss her as he had done before?

Probably.

Only it wasn't going to happen.

Ben didn't try to detain her as she got out of the car. He
waited until she'd let herself into the flat then drove away.
Anna went into the sitting room and sat on the sofa. She
closed her eyes and thought back over the day, unsurprised
when her mind immediately focused on what had happened
in the garden of Lilac Cottage. She could recall in exquisite
detail how gentle Ben's lips had been, how tender and caring.

A single tear slid down her cheek. She didn't regret that
kiss, even if he did, but she would make sure that it never
happened again. She had broken her first and only rule, the
one that said she mustn't let herself get involved, but it
wasn't too late to undo the damage.

Her eyes flew open and she felt her heart give a painful
jerk. Was it?

Anna was in her room when Eileen came to find her on
Monday morning. It was a little after eight but she had been
in the surgery for some time. It had seemed preferable to
start work rather than spend any more time thinking about
the events of the previous day. Now, as Eileen came hurrying into the room, Anna could tell at once that something
must have happened.

'What is it?' she asked, putting down her pen.

'Valerie Prentice from the playgroup has just phoned.
Evidently one of the children climbed onto the slide when
nobody was looking and fell off and hit his head,' Eileen
explained worriedly. 'She wanted to know if Adam or Ben

could pop over there to have a look at him, but neither of them has arrived yet.'

'Have you tried their mobiles?' Anna asked, frowning.

'Yes, but Adam is stuck in traffic the other side of Knutsford and Ben's phone was engaged so I just left a message. I could contact the on-call service, if you think it best,' the receptionist suggested. 'Ask them to send someone, although I don't know how long it would take. Most of their staff will be going off duty now.'

'There doesn't seem any point in doing that. By the time they send someone, Adam or Ben will have got here.' Anna frowned as she considered all their options. 'I'll go over there and take a look at the child. If I'm at all worried, I'll phone for an ambulance.'

'Would you? Thank you, dear. I'll phone Valerie back and let her know that you're on your way.' Eileen looked relieved as she hurried back to the office.

Anna fetched her jacket and left the surgery. The playgroup was held in the church hall which was only a five-minute walk away. There were a number of mums clustered in the entrance hall when she arrived, but she quickly made her way inside the building. Valerie Prentice, a capable-looking woman in her forties, greeted her with relief.

'Am I glad to see you! I wasn't sure whether I should phone for an ambulance, to be honest. I thought if one of the doctors had a look at Sam, they'd know what to do for the best.'

'I'll see how he is then decide if we need an ambulance,' Anna assured her. 'Where is he?'

'In the playroom,' Valerie told her, leading the way. She paused outside the door. 'A word of warning, though. His mother is with him and she's almost hysterical about what's happened. She isn't helping the situation one little bit.'

Anna sighed as she followed the older woman into the

room. The last thing the poor child needed was his mother going to pieces!

It turned out that the injured toddler was Sam Wilkins, the little boy who had been brought into the surgery suffering from a febrile convulsion. Anna knelt on the floor and smiled at him.

'Hello, Sam. I believe you've gone and fallen off the slide?'

The child gave a hiccuping sob then quickly buried his face in his mother's sweater. Anna turned to the young woman, inwardly sighing when she saw how terrified she looked. Quite frankly, Lucy looked a lot worse than Sam did!

'I need to have a look at his head, Lucy,' she explained softly. 'Can you turn him around to face me?'

'Do you think he might have concussion? Or brain damage even?' Lucy sounded frantic. 'I've read about how easy it is for a child to do real damage to themselves if they hit their heads.'

'I've no idea how badly injured Sam is. That's why I need to take a look at him,' Anna said firmly. 'Now, can you turn him round?'

Lucy tried to turn the child around but he started screaming and drumming his heels on the floor. To make matters worse, Lucy began crying as well. The situation was fast spiralling out of control when Janice Robertson stepped forward.

'Now, Sam, that's enough,' she said firmly. She picked him up and, to Anna's surprise, he immediately stopped crying. 'That's better. You be a good boy and let the nurse have a look at your sore head.'

Sam was as good as gold as Janice sat down on a beanbag and put him on her knee. He let Anna examine the bruise on his temple without making a murmur.

Anna smiled at him. 'That's a good boy. Now, can you tell me your name, poppet?'

'Sam,' he replied obligingly.

'Aren't you a clever boy?' she exclaimed, earning herself a tentative smile. She glanced at Lucy, who thankfully had stopped crying, although she still looked very upset. 'Did he lose consciousness at any point?'

'I don't know. I'd gone outside when it happened and one of the other mums called me back,' Lucy explained shakily.

'I was here at the time,' Janice put in. She gave the little boy a cuddle. 'I was setting out the play things in here while Valerie and Angela were marking the register. I never noticed that Sam had managed to get in here and climb up the slide. I feel so guilty about it.'

'These things happen,' Anna assured her. 'So how was Sam straight after the fall? Did he lose consciousness at any point?'

'No,' Janice stated firmly. 'He started crying immediately so I know he didn't.'

'Good.' Anna looked round as the door opened, feeling her heart lift when she saw Ben coming into the hall. He came straight over to them.

'How's he doing?' he asked, crouching down to look at the little boy. He gently turned Sam's face towards the light and grimaced when he saw the bruise on his forehead. 'Wow! What a beauty. I bet there's a great big hole in the floor where you hit it with your head.'

'Me see, me see,' Sam clamoured, leaning over to check the floor and looking disappointed when he couldn't find a hole in it.

Ben groaned as he turned to Anna. 'I keep forgetting how literally children take remarks like that. Have you found out if he lost consciousness?'

She shook her head, feeling her heart starting to race again. It was obvious that Ben must have left home in a hurry because he hadn't stopped to dry his hair and the gleaming golden strands clung damply to his head in a way that was extremely attractive. It was an effort to focus on what he was saying instead of the way her pulse was racing all of a sudden.

'He didn't. Janice was here at the time and she can vouch for that.'

'That's a good sign but I'll just check him over.' Ben reached for his case and found his torch. 'Now, Sam, I want to look into your eyes with this little light. It won't hurt so will you be a really good little boy for me?'

The child nodded uncertainly. He clung to Janice while Ben checked to see how his pupils reacted to the light. Ben switched off the torch then smiled reassuringly at Lucy.

'Everything seems to be fine. Both pupils are dilating evenly and there doesn't appear to be any indication that Sam has suffered a head injury, but I'd like you to take him to hospital just to be on the safe side. All right?'

'If you think it would be best, Doctor,' Lucy said, looking scared out of her wits.

Ben patted her shoulder. 'It's purely a precaution, Lucy. Sam is fine. Trust me.' He glanced at Anna. 'You agree, don't you?'

'I do,' she concurred, appreciating the fact that he had sought her opinion, an all-too-rare event in her experience of working with a lot of doctors.

'Will we need to go in an ambulance?' Lucy asked, looking a bit happier now that she knew that there was nothing really wrong with her son.

Ben shook his head. 'It isn't really an emergency so I can't in all honesty justify calling an ambulance. I'd offer to take you myself but I need to get back to the surgery.'

'I can take them,' Janice Robertson offered immediately. 'I've got my car outside and I'd be happy to drive them there.'

'That would be marvellous. Thanks.' Ben smiled at her, earning himself a smile in return. Anna couldn't help thinking how much better Janice looked than when she had seen her in the surgery. Working at the playgroup was obviously doing her a lot of good.

Ben phoned the hospital. Once everything was arranged, he and Anna left the church hall and got into his car.

He drove them the short distance back to the surgery and parked in the car park. 'Thanks for going over there, Anna. I appreciate it.'

'It wasn't a problem,' she assured him.

'I must have been talking to the estate agent when Eileen phoned me,' he explained, getting out of the car.

'About the cottage?' she asked, glancing at him.

'Yes.' A smile suddenly lit his face. 'My offer has been accepted! Mrs Williams had already phoned the agents and told them that she wants me to have the cottage.'

'Oh, Ben, that's wonderful news!' she declared, reaching out and hugging him. It was only when she felt his arms tightening around her that she realised what she had done, but by that point it was too late to do anything about it.

She felt him take a deep breath before he gently set her away from him and there seemed to be a new solemnity in his voice that hadn't been there moments before. 'Isn't it just? Anyway, enough of all that. It's time for work.'

He opened the surgery door for her. Anna made her way inside, trying desperately to put what had happened into perspective. She had hugged Ben purely out of excitement and he had done the same. It would be silly to read anything into it. However, all morning long she couldn't shake off the feeling that something had happened to him as he had

stood there with his arms around her. The question, of
course, was—what?

'I don't know how I made such a silly mistake! Eileen
warned me to double-check everything.'

'It's all right. Really,' Anna said soothingly. Hilary
Dwyer, their new receptionist, had somehow managed to
book two patients for the same appointment and she was
obviously distressed by her mistake.

'It isn't a hanging matter,' she teased, earning herself a
grateful smile.

'I thought you'd be cross. I mean, it's hard enough as it
is, keeping to time, without me messing up the whole system.' Hilary sighed. 'I'm here to help, not make your life
more difficult!'

'You're doing fine,' Anna assured her. 'You've only
been here for a few hours so you're bound to make the odd
mistake. Just explain to Mrs Davies that I'm running a little
late when she arrives.'

'I'll do that,' Hilary agreed, sounding relieved. She hurried away and Anna got back to writing up the notes she'd
been making. It was almost lunchtime and, assuming that
nobody turned up without an appointment, she had almost
finished her morning list. She had a free afternoon that day
and was planning on going into town to look round the
shops. She desperately needed to buy some new clothes to
wear, although the thought of spending all that money made
her heart sink. She was going to need every penny she had
to see her through the coming months.

'I just had a call from the hospital to say that Sam
Wilkins is fine.' Ben popped his head round her door and
Anna summoned a smile.

'That's great news.' She shot him a wary glance but there
was nothing about his expression as he came and perched

on the edge of her desk to hint that he felt uncomfortable about that hug they had shared. She let out her breath in a sigh of relief. It seemed that her imagination had been running away with her once again!

'I felt so sorry for Lucy,' she observed. 'She was almost out of her mind with worry.'

'I know.' Ben grimaced. 'That poor girl is a nervous wreck. I feel guilty now because it was my idea that she should take Sam to the playgroup. I thought she needed a break so I pinched your idea, although I'm not sure if it has worked as well for Lucy as it has for Janice!'

Anna laughed at his rueful expression. 'That will teach you to go meddling! Some people just have the knack of getting it right, whilst others…'

'End up by making a difficult situation worse,' he said in a tone that made her look sharply at him.

What had he meant by that? she wondered. They might have been talking about Lucy Wilkins yet she had a feeling that the remark had been more *personal* than that.

At any other time she might have asked him to explain, but she knew in her heart that it would be the wrong thing to do. Difficult though it was, she had to keep some distance between herself and Ben and not go asking him to share confidences with her.

'Anyway, I'd better be off. I've a ton of calls to do.' He got up and went to the door. 'Have a nice afternoon. What are you planning on doing?'

'Shopping.' She sighed. 'I need some new clothes. I'm not going to be able to fit into my old ones for very much longer.'

His eyes swooped down her body, clad in the sobre, navy blue uniform dress. 'It's going to be rather costly, isn't it? Plus you've got all the stuff to buy for the baby as well.'

'I'll manage,' she assured him, although she wasn't sure how.

'Look, Anna, if you need any cash…'

'I don't,' she said quickly, knowing what he was going to say. Although she appreciated his kindness, there was no way that she could borrow money from him.

Ben shrugged. 'The offer's there if you want to take me up on it at any time. I'll see you later.'

Anna sighed as he left. It had been kind of him to offer to lend her some money but he didn't understand her true circumstances. Once she finished working at the surgery she would have only state benefits to live off apart from a few savings. There was no way that she could borrow money because she wouldn't be able to pay it back.

It brought it home to her how difficult the coming months were going to be. Bringing up a child on her own wasn't something she had planned on doing, but she just had to make the best of the situation. There wasn't going to be any handsome prince riding up on his white charger to carry *her* off!

She smiled sadly. She had never wanted a prince, in all honesty. All she had ever wanted had been the right man to love her. The chances of that happening now were very slim, though. Few men would be interested in a woman in her situation. Even if they could accept that she had a child, could they accept the way it had been conceived? Surrogacy was so far beyond most people's experience that a lot of men would have difficulty dealing with the idea.

Ben had accepted it, though, a small voice whispered. And he hadn't been shocked. He didn't seem to find what she had done anything to be ashamed of. His response had been everything that she could have wished for, and it was unsettling to realise that she would measure every man she met against him.

* * *

Another week passed and Anna knew that she couldn't hide her pregnancy for much longer. She was now over four months pregnant and her body was changing daily. Her breasts had grown noticeably heavier, her nipples enlarging and darkening. Her stomach was swelling as the baby grew inside her and her waistline thickening so that the elasticated belt that she wore for work dug into her uncomfortably. In the end, she simply plucked up her courage and went into the office and told Eileen and Hilary that she was having a baby.

'I did wonder.' Eileen smiled kindly at her. 'I've had two of my own so you tend to spot the signs, if you know what I mean.'

'I do.' Anna smiled gamely, waiting for all the questions that were bound to follow. She wasn't sure what she intended to tell the two receptionists and had decided to play it by ear.

In the event, neither woman said very much. Anna was left with the impression that they were trying to be tactful. Maybe they believed that she had been left in the lurch, which wasn't all that far from the truth. However, she had to admit to feeling relieved when she left the office. Although she didn't mind Ben and Adam knowing the truth, she preferred to keep the circumstances surrounding the baby's conception to herself.

'You look deep in thought. Problems?' Ben was coming out of the staffroom, carrying a cup of coffee, and he paused when he saw her.

'Not really,' she replied, struggling to stop her pulse performing its customary surge at the sight of him. It was a trick it had started doing the previous week and she was doing her best to cure it of the habit. She focused instead on what he had said and explained what had happened, rather surprised when he frowned.

'You haven't done anything to be ashamed of, Anna.'

'I'm not ashamed. I'm just wary about telling people the truth in case they don't understand.'

'It isn't difficult. You set out to help your sister and ended up being let down through no fault of your own. Those are the facts and they seem quite straightforward to me.'

She sighed when she heard the bite in his voice. He sounded annoyed and she wasn't sure why. 'I know and I really appreciate it, Ben. It's just that other people might not see the situation so clearly as you do. I have to think about the baby. I don't want his or her life made any more difficult because people are shocked about its background.'

'I understand that. But what are you going to tell the child when it's growing up? You aren't going to lie, I hope?'

'Of course not!' she shot back, hurt that he should have imagined she would do a thing like that. 'I want this child to know just how special he is and understand how much his natural mother wanted him, or her, of course.'

'It won't be easy,' he warned bluntly.

'I know it won't. It's a lot for any child to take in, but I don't intend to avoid the issue even if it is difficult. I just don't understand why you doubt that I shall do it.'

'Bitter experience.' His tone was clipped.

'Experience?' she repeated, then sighed as she realised what he had meant. 'You told me that your mother was a single parent. Did she not tell you anything about your background?'

'No. I had to find out most of the details myself. I would have preferred it if I had been told the truth as soon as I was old enough to understand.'

She hated to hear the echo of old pain in his voice.

'Maybe she found it too difficult to talk about,' she suggested quietly.

'I'm sure you're right.' He summoned a smile. 'But take my advice and don't try to keep secrets from this child, Anna. It's best to be completely honest from the beginning.'

'I shall.' She shrugged, hoping that he believed her. It seemed important that she should make him understand her reasoning because it might help convince him. 'I know it seems illogical to you, but I just don't want to say too much at the moment. Once the baby is born, I'm hoping that the situation will become easier.'

'I think you'll find that folk are far more sympathetic than you imagine. Don't let what that nurse and your brother-in-law said influence you, Anna.'

'I hadn't realised that I was,' she admitted truthfully.

'I think it has been playing on your mind. It's understandable because you have so much to cope with at the moment. Just remember that I'm here if you need someone to talk things over with.'

'I shall. Thanks, Ben,' she said softly. She went back to the treatment room, thinking about what he had said. She couldn't deny that she was touched by his obvious desire to help her.

She sighed as it hit her how wonderful it would be to turn to Ben over the coming months, to seek support and reassurance whenever she was worried. However, she had to avoid letting herself rely on him too much. It would be far too easy to let friendship slip into something more, or it would for her any way. When she left Winton in a few months' time, she didn't want to leave with a broken heart.

CHAPTER SEVEN

'I KNOW we've a long way to go before we reach our goal, but I'm confident that we'll get there.'

It was Friday morning, over two weeks later, and everyone was gathered in the staffroom. Adam had scheduled a meeting after morning surgery and had just finished telling them about his plans to expand the practice.

Anna had to confess that she'd found the proposals he had made to turn the surgery into a health centre very exciting. Obviously, the area health authority would need to be consulted before they could apply for the appropriate funding. She couldn't help thinking wistfully how wonderful it would have been to have played a part in the expansion scheme.

'What's the long face for? Don't you like the idea of the surgery becoming a fully fledged health centre?'

She smiled as Ben came over to her. 'Of course I do. I was just wishing that I'd be here to see all the exciting new changes that are going to take place.'

'Why don't you ask Adam if there's any chance of you doing part-time work after the baby is born? We are going to need more than one practice nurse with all the extra clinics and longer opening hours.'

He glanced round as Adam joined them, not giving her time to say how she felt about the idea. 'I was just saying to Anna that we'll need more than one practice nurse once the health centre is up and running. I suggested that she might be able to work here on a part-time basis after the baby is born. What do you think?'

'That it sounds like a great idea to me,' Adam said immediately. 'How would you feel about it, Anna?'

'I don't know,' she said slowly, then flushed when she realised how ungracious that must have sounded. It wasn't that she didn't appreciate the offer, but she couldn't help wondering if it would be the right thing to do. Would it really be wise to continue working with Ben when it would mean that she got even more used to having him around?

It was difficult to answer that question and impossible to tell either Adam or Ben why she had reservations about the idea. She opted for a small distortion of the truth instead. 'Obviously, I'd love to stay on here, but a lot would depend on whether I could find anywhere to live. Winton is a very expensive place and I really can't see me being able to afford to live in the town.'

'I can understand that,' Adam agreed sympathetically. 'Still, the offer's there if you want to think about it. I'm more than satisfied with your work and the way you've fitted in here so well. I would hate to lose you if there's a chance that you might be able to stay on.'

'Thank you,' Anna said quietly.

'Anyway, this might be putting the cart before the horse but how would you two feel about coming over to lunch on Sunday to celebrate our new venture?' Adam grinned. 'Beth has been nagging me for weeks about inviting you over so that she can meet you, Anna.'

'Sounds like a great idea to me,' Ben declared before she could answer. 'It's been ages since I saw Beth. It would be nice to catch up on what's been happening to her.'

'Not a lot, I'm afraid.' Adam sighed. 'She's been stuck at home for most of the time because Hannah isn't allowed to go anywhere she might come into contact with germs.' He glanced at Anna and she couldn't help noticing the expression of love on his face. 'My daughter has had a bone-marrow transplant for leukaemia, in case you didn't know.'

'Ben mentioned something about it a few weeks ago. How is she doing?' she asked in genuine concern.

'Marvellously. You wouldn't believe the transformation in her. It's Beth I feel sorry for because she's stuck in the house so much of the time, not that she complains, mind. She'll be thrilled to know that you two are coming over on Sunday.'

Adam gave them a broad smile and Anna didn't have the heart to tell him that she hadn't decided whether she should accept the invitation. She sighed as he moved away to speak to Hilary. These were kind people, people she liked and admired, and in other circumstances she would have welcomed their friendship, but she had to remember her rule about not getting too involved. It was going to be hard enough to walk away when the job came to an end.

She glanced at Ben and felt a small explosion of pain in the region of her heart. It was going to be very hard indeed.

Anna decided to wear one of her new dresses for lunch that Sunday. Although it hadn't been expensive, she knew that it suited her. Made from a soft midnight-blue fabric lightly sprinkled with a pattern of tiny pink rosebuds, the dress skimmed her figure, just hinting at the curves beneath. There was a deep pleat down the front which would give room for expansion in the coming months, but she didn't think that it looked too much like a maternity dress at the present time.

She had pinned up her hair into a loose knot on the crown of her head and the sophisticated style suited her, showing off her slender neck and small ears. She didn't own much jewellery but a pair of tiny imitation pearl studs in her lobes added a touch of elegance. She had taken extra care with her make-up as well, smoothing a pale base coat over her skin and adding a hint of blusher to her cheek-bones and a touch of rose-pink lipstick to her mouth. All things considered, she didn't think she looked too bad, but what would Ben think when he saw her?

The thought slid into her mind before she could stop it and she sighed when she saw the troubled light that had appeared in her eyes. It shouldn't have mattered a jot what Ben thought about her appearance but there was no point lying to herself. She wanted to look nice for him but it was the reason why that worried her most.

If Ben was simply her friend then surely she wouldn't have felt this need to look attractive for him? It made her realise that her feelings towards him were altering and that she was beginning to think of him as more than a friend, yet what point was there in letting that happen? Even if Ben reciprocated her feelings, she would never take the risk of letting the situation develop. She was having another woman's child. It wouldn't be fair to burden him with that kind of a responsibility!

By the time Ben arrived a short time later, Anna was dreading the coming afternoon. Fortunately, he didn't appear to notice her abstraction as they drove to Adam's house, and once they were there there simply wasn't time to brood. Beth greeted them at the door and swept them inside, looking so pleased to see them that Anna's spirits immediately lifted. It seemed silly to start worrying about something that hadn't even happened!

'Drinks first then we can eat.' Beth shooed them into the living room and got them seated. 'What would you like? You name it—'

'And we probably haven't got it,' Adam chipped in. He looped an arm around Beth's shoulders and Anna couldn't help but feel touched when she saw the look of love that passed between them.

'Confession time, folks. I forgot to go to the supermarket on my way home yesterday so you can blame me for the lack of choice.' He dropped a kiss on the end of Beth's nose. 'Too eager to get home, I'm afraid.'

Beth laughed. 'Oh, what a smooth talker you are, Adam Knight! You should be in the diplomatic service. However, in view of your disgraceful dereliction of duty it appears that it's going to have to be wine or soft drinks. Sorry.'

Anna laughed. 'It's not a problem. I'd love some orange juice, if you have it.'

'We do. How about you, Ben? A glass of wine suit you?' Adam asked easily, unfazed by the fact that the choice was so limited.

'Fine. I'm driving anyway so I won't be drinking much,' Ben said comfortably. 'And Anna can't drink because of the baby.'

'So that lets you off the hook, doesn't it, Mr Forgetful?' Beth teased, earning herself another quick kiss. She sighed as Adam left the room to fetch their drinks. 'Actually, it's no wonder he forgot about the drinks. I have to leave him to do most of the shopping and it can't be easy, remembering everything after a hard day at work.'

'Adam told me about Hannah,' Anna put in. 'I imagine that your time away from the house has been rather limited recently.'

'Tell me about it!' Beth groaned, flopping down onto a chair and kicking off her shoes. 'I'm developing a severe case of cabin fever but it's been worth it. Hannah's consultant told me on Friday afternoon that she should be able to go back to school just before Christmas.'

'That's brilliant news!' Ben declared.

'Isn't it just,' Beth began, then stopped as the door

opened and a little girl shyly crept into the room. 'Come and say hello, darling,' she urged, holding out her hand to the child. 'You know Uncle Ben, and this is Anna who works at the surgery with him and Daddy.'

Anna smiled as Hannah stared at her with huge, solemn blue eyes. She couldn't help thinking how adorable the child was with her halo of soft black curls. 'Hello, Hannah. It's lovely to meet you.'

'Hello,' the child murmured, then hurried over to Beth and squeezed onto the chair beside her.

'I brought you some of those cards that you love to swop,' Ben told her, taking a couple of foil-wrapped packets out of his pocket.

Hannah's face instantly lit up. 'Oh, thank you, Uncle Ben!' She knelt on the floor beside him and quickly opened the packets, exclaiming in delight when she saw the cards. 'I haven't got *any* of these.'

Anna couldn't help noticing that the child wasn't at all shy with Ben, but she'd noticed before that he had a wonderful way around children. Fortunately, Adam came back with their drinks just then and in the ensuing hubbub she had no time to dwell on the thought, let alone wonder why it made her feel a little sad. The thought that Ben wouldn't be around to develop a relationship with her child after it was born wasn't something she wanted to think about.

Beth served lunch in the conservatory a short time later and Anna enjoyed the company as much as she enjoyed the delicious roast beef that was served. It was good to be surrounded by so many nice people, people who seemed to have accepted her. She helped Beth carry the dirty dishes into the kitchen after they had finished the main course, pausing when the other woman turned to her.

'I just wanted to tell you how much I admire what you're

doing, Anna. Adam told me about the baby and everything, and I think you're simply wonderful.'

'Why, thank you,' Anna replied, feeling a lump come to her throat.

'Oh, dear, I hope I haven't upset you,' Beth exclaimed in concern. 'That was the last thing I intended to do.'

'No, of course not... Well, I'm not really upset, just touched,' Anna confessed honestly. 'I've been wary of telling people the truth about the baby because I wasn't sure how they would react. It is rather an unusual situation.'

'It is and that just proves how brave you are,' Beth assured her. 'Not many women would have done what you've done.'

'That's what Ben keeps saying,' she admitted, then flushed when she heard the wistful note in her voice.

Beth picked up the plates and started loading them into the dishwasher. 'Adam mentioned that you and Ben seem to get along extremely well,' she said artlessly.

'We do. He's a good friend,' Anna agreed, trying her best to keep her tone level. She bit her lip when the other woman treated her to an old-fashioned look.

'Just a friend?'

'Yes, that's all.' She took a deep breath and looked Beth firmly in the eye. 'It's more than enough in the circumstances, wouldn't you say?'

'Meaning that you don't intend to let the situation develop into anything more because of the baby?' Beth shrugged. 'Does Ben know that? I was watching him while we were eating and it's obvious how fond he is of you, Anna.'

'I'm fond of him, too—as a friend,' she added quickly, needing to make sure that Beth understood the facts.

'Well, so long as you both know the score, that's fine.' Beth didn't say anything more on the subject, switching the conversation to the plans for the surgery instead. However, Anna couldn't put the conversation out of her mind no matter how hard she tried.

Was Ben fond of her? And if so was it just as a friend or…?

Her mind stalled at that point. She didn't want to think what the *or* might be.

'It's been lovely meeting you. Thank you for coming.'

'Thank you for inviting me. I've really enjoyed it,' Anna replied truthfully, returning Beth's hug.

'You must come again,' Beth replied. 'Both of you.'

Anna sighed when she saw the pointed look the other woman gave her. It was obvious that she hadn't managed to convince Beth that she and Ben were just good friends. Was it any wonder, though? she found herself thinking, when she was having such problems believing it herself. All afternoon long the thought that Ben might want to be more than just her friend had whirled round and round in her head, but it would be a mistake to let herself get carried away by the idea.

'A very enjoyable day, wouldn't you say?' Ben glanced at her as she got into the car. 'You and Beth seemed to get on well together.'

'We did.' Anna summoned a smile, not wanting him to suspect that there was anything wrong. She had known from the outset that their relationship had to be kept within strict boundaries so it was foolish to wish that things could have been different. 'I really like Beth. She's so warm and friendly.'

'Beth's a very kind and caring woman, and she absolutely adores Hannah and Adam,' he agreed warmly, turning the car around so that they could head back to Winton.

'The feeling is obviously mutual,' Anna observed softly.

'It doesn't take a clairvoyant to see that Adam is crazy about her.'

'No, it doesn't. They're very lucky, aren't they?'

She looked at him and frowned. 'Lucky?'

'That they've found each another,' he explained. 'A lot of people go through life without ever meeting that one special person.'

'Or they meet them at entirely the wrong time,' she said without thinking, then felt herself colour.

'Are you speaking from experience?' he asked, and she couldn't help but hear the grating note in his voice.

'It was just a generalisation. How's the negotiations for the cottage going, by the way?' she asked, quickly changing the subject. She could scarcely believe that she had said something so revealing and could only hope that Ben hadn't read too much into the chance remark.

Had it been a chance remark, though? a small voice whispered. Or had it been a simple statement of fact? If she had met Ben at a different point in her life, wouldn't their relationship be very different?

'My solicitor seems fairly confident that we should be able to exchange contracts by the end of next month,' he replied evenly.

'Th-that's good,' she said, struggling to focus on what he was saying rather than her own wayward thoughts. The thought that she and Ben could have been more than friends if she hadn't been pregnant was so bitter-sweet that it made her heart ache. 'You should be able to move in before Christmas, then, I expect.'

'I'm hoping so, not that Christmas is much of an event in my life.' He shrugged when she looked quizzically at him. 'It's not much fun celebrating on your own, is it?'

'I suppose not,' she agreed, her face falling when she remembered the previous Christmas. She had spent it with

Jo and it had been a very happy time for both of them because they'd just learned that they had been accepted for IVF treatment. She couldn't help thinking how different it was going to be that year.

'I didn't mean to make you feel miserable,' Ben apologised.

'I know you didn't.' She summoned a smile. 'It's just that last Christmas Jo and I were at the planning stage, wondering how long it would take before I got pregnant and if the baby would be a boy or a girl.' She shrugged. 'It was all so exciting.'

'And this Christmas will be just as wonderful because the baby is a reality.' He laid his hand gently on her stomach. 'You're carrying Jo's hopes and dreams inside you, Anna, and that will make this a Christmas to remember.'

She was so moved by what he'd said that she felt her eyes fill with tears, and he groaned. 'Me and my big mouth! I'm obviously suffering from a severe case of foot-in-mouth disease.'

His expression was so comical that she couldn't help laughing and she saw him smile. 'That's better. I love seeing you laugh like that, Anna. It's like watching the sun come out.'

There was a throbbing note in his voice which turned the remark into something else, something that made her bones feel like liquid all of a sudden. Anna raised shocked eyes to his face and felt her heart come to a halt when she saw the way he was looking at her with such hunger, such need.

There was a moment when she thought that he was going to do or say something before he returned his attention to the road, and for the rest of the journey the conversation was kept strictly to neutral topics. However, it was a relief when they reached the surgery at last. Although the conversation had been low-key, the atmosphere inside the car had grown increasingly tense so that she could hardly wait to make her escape.

'I'll see you tomorrow, then, Anna,' he said, drawing the car to a halt and turning to her.

'Yes.' It was an effort to keep her voice level and she saw him frown.

'Look, Anna, maybe—'

'Thanks for the lift.' She didn't let him finish as she quickly opened the car door. In her heart she knew that it would be a mistake. Ben might say something which he later regretted and she...well, she didn't have the right to hope for anything more than she already had.

She went up to the flat and let herself in, not looking back to wave as he drove away. She went straight to her bedroom and put her coat away then made herself a cup of tea.

She took it into the sitting room and turned on the television, using the familiar everyday actions to distract herself. She didn't want to think about what had happened, wouldn't allow herself to wonder what Ben might have said. It was too dangerous to start dreaming about something she couldn't have.

'So Dr Cole has left it up to me to decide if I want to go on HRT. To be honest, I've felt so much better lately that I don't think I need any pills.'

Anna smiled. She'd been on her way to the office when she'd spotted Janice Robertson leaving Ben's room and they'd stopped to have a chat. 'It's entirely up to you. Although a lot of women find that they cope much better with the menopause if they have hormone replacement therapy, not everyone needs it.'

'That's what Dr Cole said.' Janice sighed ruefully. 'To

think that I'd been putting off having those blood tests *and* coming for the results because I didn't want to admit that I was going through the change. It seems daft now but at the time it made perfect sense. I couldn't bear the thought that my days of having children were coming to an end because it made me feel as though there was no point to my life any longer.'

'It's very easy to get things out of proportion when you're feeling low,' Anna assured her, then frowned.

Had she got what had happened on Sunday out of proportion? she wondered. In the past three days Ben hadn't given any sign that he wanted to further their relationship, yet on Sunday she would have put good money on it.

'That's why working at the playgroup has been such a lifesaver,' Janice declared. 'It's really given me a lift.'

Anna quickly returned her thoughts to the conversation and smiled. 'I'm so glad. It's obvious that you're great with the children. I could see how little Sam Wilkins adores you.'

Janice grimaced. 'I felt a bit awful about that, actually. I hope that Lucy didn't think that I was trying to take over from her. I know how hard she tries with Sam, and how much she worries about him.'

'I'm sure she was glad of your help,' Anna assured her. 'Anyway, I'm really pleased that everything is working out so well for you, Janice.'

'Thanks. And thanks for putting me in touch with the playgroup in the first place.' Janice patted her arm. 'If you ever need anyone to babysit when the time comes, feel free to call on me!'

'I appreciate the offer, although I don't know if I'll be staying in Winton,' Anna explained.

'Oh, I hope you do!' Janice exclaimed. 'We'll all miss

you if you leave. Surely you could return here to work after the baby's born?'

'Maybe,' she replied noncommittally. She sighed as Janice left. She couldn't help thinking how hard it was going to be, moving somewhere else. She would know nobody and have no friends to turn to.

That thought naturally brought her back to Ben and she groaned. What was that saying about all roads leading to Rome? Substitute Ben's name for the name of the city and it fitted perfectly!

Anna was in the flat, making herself some lunch, when there was a knock on the door. She hurried to answer it, feeling her heart sink when she saw Ben standing outside and realised how grim he looked.

'Is something wrong?' she asked, opening the door so that he could step inside the tiny hall.

'I've just had Valerie Prentice on the phone,' he told her without any preamble. 'Lucy Wilkins hasn't turned up to collect Sam from playgroup and she wondered if I had any idea where she might be. Evidently, Lucy had mentioned something about making an appointment to see me this morning, but Eileen assures me that she didn't phone up.'

'Where on earth can she be?' Anna exclaimed worriedly. 'It isn't like her not to be there for Sam. If anything, she's over-protective.'

'I know. That's why I'm so worried.' He sounded really concerned. 'I'm going round to where she lives to see if she's all right. I know it sounds silly but I have this funny feeling that something might have happened to her.'

'I'll go with you,' Anna said immediately.

'Would you? Thanks.' He smiled at her and once again she couldn't fail to see the warmth in his eyes.

She turned away, using the excuse that she needed to

fetch her coat, but that was all it was—an excuse. She was simply trying to avoid having to deal with what was happening, but one day soon she would have to face up to it. And when she did she had to make sure that she did the right thing by Ben even if it wasn't what she really wanted. She wouldn't do anything that might end up hurting him.

It didn't take them long to drive to Lucy's bedsit above a fish-and-chip shop in one of the poorest areas of the town. Anna grimaced as she got out of the car and had to step over a pile of litter that was scattered across the pavement.

'I didn't realise that there were areas like this in Winton,' she confessed.

'This estate was built in the sixties as an overspill area for the city,' Ben explained grimly. 'It was the trend at the time. The logic behind it was that the two communities would integrate and the poorer folk would strive to improve themselves. The reality is that it's hard to change your lifestyle if you've not got the money or the resources to do so.'

'It must be,' she agreed, following him into the chip shop. Ben went straight to the counter and quickly introduced himself to the proprietor then asked him if he had seen Lucy that day. Anna had guessed what the answer was from the man's negative shake of his head before Ben came to report back to her.

'He hasn't seen her for a couple of days, apparently. However, he says that isn't unusual because she tends to keep very much to herself.'

'So what are we going to do now?' she asked worriedly.

'We'll go up to the flat and knock to see if she's in. If we don't get a reply, we'll need to consider our options,' he explained flatly.

Anna shivered because she, too, was starting to get a bad

feeling about this. They made their way up a narrow staircase at the rear of the shop and knocked on the door at the top, but there was no reply.

Ben pressed his ear to the door. 'I can hear music playing so she must be in there.'

He knocked again, harder this time, but he still didn't get an answer. Anna could tell that he was growing increasingly concerned and wasn't surprised when he curtly told her that he was going down to the shop to see if there was a spare key available.

He came back with the owner of the chip shop, who unlocked the door. Anna just had time to take stock of the shabby furniture and peeling paintwork before her gaze alighted on the figure lying on a narrow single bed. She felt her heart turn over with fear when she realised that it was Lucy.

Ben uttered something rough as he ran across the room. Bending down, he quickly checked the girl's pulse then picked up a small brown bottle that was lying on the floor beside the bed and started firing out instructions. 'Phone for an ambulance. Tell them that it's a paracetamol overdose.'

He turned to Anna as the owner of the shop hurried away. 'We need to get her on her feet. Can you help me? She's been drinking from the look of it. That's why she's passed out.'

'Of course.' Anna's heart was racing as she hurried to the bed. The girl was muttering incoherently and there was a strong smell of alcohol on her breath. There was an empty bottle of cheap wine on the bedside table as well as a few paracetamol tablets, although there was no way of knowing just how many Lucy might have taken.

Ben glanced at the tablets and his tone was grim. 'It takes very few paracetamol tablets to kill a person. Paracetamol destroys the liver unless the antidote is given. I've heard of people being sent home from hospital, apparently well, then turning up a few days later with liver failure.'

He hauled Lucy to her feet and placed her arm around his shoulders. 'Can you go round the other side, Anna? We'll try to walk her round until the ambulance gets here.'

'Do you think she'll be all right?' she asked, unable to keep the catch out of her voice.

'If she gets the right treatment, she should have a chance, but there are no guarantees. Why the hell did she do such a crazy thing?'

'Because she was desperate. Because it was the only thing she could think of when everything else had failed,' she said sadly.

'Then there has to be something seriously wrong with a society that leaves a kid like this to struggle on her own, that's all I can say,' Ben snapped. He sounded furiously angry but Anna knew that his anger was simply an outlet. Ben really cared about the poor girl. He cared deeply because he was that sort of person, and something inside her blossomed at the thought.

The ambulance arrived ten minutes later and the two paramedics quickly carried Lucy downstairs. Ben turned to Anna as the paramedics loaded the teenager on board.

'I'm going with them. I want to make sure that she gets the correct treatment. Will you explain to Adam what's happened and tell him that I'll be back as soon as I can?'

'Of course,' she agreed immediately.

He felt in his pocket and handed her some money. 'Take a taxi back to the surgery. I'm sorry to leave you in the lurch like this...'

'I'll be fine,' she assured him, seeing the concern in his eyes.

'Take care, Anna.' He bent and kissed her swiftly on the mouth then got into his car as the ambulance pulled away.

Anna pressed a trembling hand to her lips, feeling little shivers working their way through her body. 'Take care,' he'd said, and it was such a cliché nowadays, the sort of thing that people tagged onto the end of a conversation without really thinking about it. However, it was the way that he'd said it which would linger on in her mind long after the actual words had faded. She could have built a whole future on the tone of his voice if she'd let herself do something so foolish.

CHAPTER EIGHT

ANNA asked the taxi driver to drop her off at the church hall instead of going straight back to the surgery. Arrangements would need to be made to ensure that Sam was cared for while Lucy was in hospital. Valerie Prentice met her at the door.

'What's happened? Have you found out where Lucy is?'

Anna quickly explained what had happened, sighing when she saw how upset Valerie was. 'I know exactly how you feel. I only wish I'd realised that Lucy was so desperate.'

Valerie wiped her eyes with a tissue. 'That poor kid! It doesn't bear thinking about, what might have happened if you hadn't found her.'

'It doesn't. But what we have to decide now is what to do about Sam,' she said. 'I suppose the correct procedure in a case like this would be to contact the social services department—'

'Oh, do we have to?' Valerie put in. 'Sam will be terrified if a bunch of strangers come here and take him away.'

'I realise that,' Anna admitted. 'But what's the alternative? I don't know how long Lucy will be in hospital and, to be honest, I don't think she will be fit to look after him on her own when she comes out. She is going to need a lot of emotional support as well as practical help in the coming months.'

'I wonder if Janice would look after him?' Valerie suggested. 'Don't get me wrong, I'm more than happy to take care of Sam but he really loves Janice. He might find it less upsetting if she took him home with her. Let's see what she thinks about the idea.'

Valerie briskly led the way into the hall where Janice and Sam were sitting on a beanbag, reading a story. They both looked up expectantly when Anna and Valerie entered the room.

'Have you found Lucy?' Janice mouthed over the top of the child's head.

Anna nodded, not wanting to say too much in front of the child. Valerie murmured something about giving Sam a drink and whisked him away to the kitchen while Anna told Janice what had happened.

'I feel so guilty!' Janice exclaimed. 'I knew that Lucy was finding it difficult to cope, but I didn't realise just how bad things must have got.'

'I feel exactly the same,' Anna said sadly. 'But what we have to concentrate on now is making sure that Sam is taken care of. Valerie suggested that you might be kind enough to look after him. I'll have to inform the social services department about what's happened, so they will arrange a carer for him if you'd rather not do it.'

'Of course I'll look after him,' Janice said immediately. 'I'll be happy to. How long will Lucy be in hospital, do you think?'

'I'm not sure. Dr Cole went with her to make sure that she received the correct treatment. Evidently, there's an antidote to paracetamol poisoning. But I've no idea how long they will keep her in.'

'Well, I'll look after Sam for however long it takes. Maybe we can tell the social services department that I'm a friend of his mother's?' Janice grimaced. 'Some friend to have let such a dreadful thing happen to a young girl like that.'

'It wasn't your fault, Janice,' she assured her, although she knew exactly how Janice felt.

Once the arrangements had been finalised Anna returned to the surgery and briefly explained to a shocked Eileen and Hilary what had happened. It was obvious that they were as upset as everyone else was by the affair. Anna couldn't help wishing that they'd all had the foresight to do something before rather than after the event. She mentioned it to Adam when she went to tell him where Ben was, but he shook his head.

'There's no point blaming yourself because you weren't to know this would happen. Most attempted suicides aren't planned. Maybe something happened this morning and Lucy simply couldn't see any way round the problem, and that's why she did such a silly thing.'

'I knew how hard she was finding it to cope, though,' Anna said, still troubled. She sighed. 'I, more than anyone, should have known how difficult her circumstances were because I'm going to be in the same boat in a few months' time.'

'But you are a grown woman who can deal with the situation, Anna. You also have people around you who care what happens to you,' Adam said quietly. 'That makes a big difference.'

She smiled gratefully at him. 'I suppose it does. Thanks for reminding me.'

He got up and gave her a friendly hug. 'Don't mention it. Anyway, I'm only standing in for Ben. *He* most certainly would have told you how silly you are to compare yourself to Lucy!'

She coloured when she heard the teasing note in his voice. Had Beth said something to him about her and Ben? she found herself wondering. Or had he simply reached the same conclusion by himself?

The thought that Adam also believed that Ben was fond of her seemed to add extra weight to the idea, yet it left her in a quandary. She would be lying if she claimed that she didn't like the idea, but in her heart she knew that it would be wrong to encourage his feelings. The last thing she wanted was for Ben to get any more deeply involved when it would affect his whole life. At the end of the day, this child was her responsibility, not his.

It was almost time for evening surgery before Ben got back. Anna was in the kitchen, making herself a cup of tea, when he appeared.

'Hi. I'm back at last.'

'How's Lucy?' Anna demanded anxiously.

'Feeling extremely sorry for herself but, thankfully, out of danger.' He sank onto a chair and heaved a sigh. 'I don't want to have to go through anything like that again in a hurry!'

'No wonder.' Anna made a second cup of tea and placed it in front of him. 'Drink that up. You look worn out.'

'I am. I think it's a combination of worry and good old hunger,' he admitted ruefully. His stomach chose that particular moment to grumble and he grimaced. 'Told you.'

'Didn't you have anything to eat while you were at the hospital?' she asked worriedly, thinking how exhausted he looked.

'There wasn't time.' He took a sip of the tea. 'The doctor on duty in the casualty department wanted to treat Lucy with activated charcoal when he found out that she'd taken a drug overdose. I had to kick up a real stink before he agreed to use acetylcysteine, the recommended antidote for paracetamol poisoning.'

'Really?' Anna couldn't hide her surprise.

'Really. I don't know how long the guy has been working in accident and emergency care—he's a locum, evidently—but he definitely needs to brush up on his facts. There are national guidelines laid down for the use of acetylcysteine in cases of paracetamol poisoning. Provided it is administered within ten hours of ingesting the drug, the patient should recover and not subsequently suffer liver failure,' he explained grimly.

'Anyway, I had a word with the hospital manager before I left and left him in little doubt of my feelings on the matter. I also intend to follow it up with a letter to the board of trustees. It's totally unacceptable that people could die because they aren't given the correct treatment, although it would be a damn site better if it had never happened in the first place.'

Anna sighed when she heard the regret in his voice. She knew that Ben was blaming himself for not having guessed what Lucy was planning. Unfortunately, there was no time to reassure him that he wasn't at fault in any way because the first patients had arrived for evening surgery. However, she suspected that none of them would forget what Lucy had done for a long time to come.

Ben looked quite grey with fatigue when he came into the office after surgery ended. Anna felt really worried about him. He still hadn't had anything to eat and she hated to think of him having to trek all the way home and start cooking for himself. It spurred her into making an offer that she certainly wouldn't have made otherwise.

'How do you fancy coming up to the flat and letting me cook you some supper? I've a couple of lamb chops going begging.'

He looked at her quizzically. 'That's very kind of you, but to what do I owe such a generous offer?'

'To the fact that you look like one of the walking dead,

I imagine,' Eileen chipped in, coming into the office. 'You look as though you're in desperate need of a bit of TLC, so you'd be a fool to refuse, if you want my opinion.'

'In that case, what can I say except that I would be delighted to accept?' Ben grinned, his brown eyes twinkling with laughter. 'Lamb chops served with a side order of TLC sounds very tempting to me, Anna.'

'Oh, good. I…I'll go and put the chops under the grill, then,' she murmured, hurrying to the door. 'Come up whenever you're ready.'

She took a deep breath as she reached the relative sanctuary of the hall but it did little to calm her nerves. Lamb chops and TLC indeed! She was starting to have serious misgivings about her impulsive offer but there was no way that she could back out of it now.

The chops were already cooking and she'd made a crisp spinach salad to go with them by the time Ben arrived. She had left the door on the latch so he came straight into the kitchen and looked around. 'Want any help?'

'No, it's fine. I'm just going to microwave these potatoes.' Anna popped a couple of large baking potatoes into the microwave and set the timer then turned, jumping when she almost bumped into him.

'Sorry.' He held up his hands in front of him. 'I didn' mean to get under your feet. I was just going to lay the table for you, seeing that you have the cooking all under control.'

'Oh, right, thanks. Do you know where everything is?' she asked shakily, struggling to make her stupid heart behave itself. It felt as though it were aiming for a gold medal from the speed it was racing, yet she couldn't understand why she was so nervous all of a sudden.

'I'm sure I can find everything I need,' he replied evenly.

'In that case, I'll go and change out of this uniform,' she

told him, and quickly made her escape. She hurried into
the bedroom and after a moment's deliberation changed
into the dress she had worn for Sunday lunch at Adam's
house. She zipped it up then picked up a brush to tidy her
hair. It had come loose from the French pleat she'd worn
that day, so she took out all the hairpins and brushed it
until it hung in a silken cloud around her shoulders.

She put the brush back on the dressing-table then took a
deep breath when she saw the glitter of excitement in her
eyes. Ben is just going to have supper, she told herself
sternly. There isn't anything more complicated to it than
that. Yet no matter how many times she repeated the words
they didn't seem to help.

'I've turned the chops over and the timer on the microwave has pinged so the potatoes are done,' he informed her
when she went back to the kitchen. He had loosened his
tie and rolled up the sleeves of his grey shirt, and he looked
completely at ease as he prodded the chops with a fork.
'Have a look at these and see if you think they're ready.'

Anna sidled past him and peered into the grill. 'They
look fine to me. You sit down and I'll serve up.'

'How about something to drink?' he suggested, opening
the fridge. He lifted out a bottle of sparkling apple juice
and grinned at her. 'We can pretend this is champagne.'

'*You* might be able to but my imagination isn't *that*
good,' she retorted, carefully lifting the hot grill pan out
and placing it on a trivet. She slid a couple of chops onto
each plate then took the potatoes out of the microwave and
split them down the middle. 'Butter or sour cream dressing?' she asked, glancing at him.

'Both, please.' He grinned wickedly. 'My excuse is that
I need the extra calories because I'm starving!'

'Oh, what it must be like not to have to watch your

weight,' she declared, opening the fridge and getting out the butter and a jar of sour cream dressing. 'I envy you.'

'I don't know why. You have the best excuse in the world for putting on weight at the moment.' His smile was teasing, his dark brown eyes laughing up at her as she put the plate in front of him.

'I don't know about that. It won't do me or the baby any good if I end up as big as a house,' she said crisply, because she didn't enjoy the way her heart was behaving once again. It was the way that Ben was looking at her, his eyes like warm brown velvet as he smiled at her. It would have needed a far harder heart than hers not to respond.

'I don't think there's much danger of that,' he assured her, adding an extremely generous dollop of the dressing to his potato. He forked up a mouthful then closed his eyes. 'Delicious. Genuine manna from heaven!'

Anna laughed. 'A man of simple tastes, obviously.'

'I am, but, then, I'm a simple kind of guy. I can't see any point in making life complicated.'

She wasn't sure what he had meant by that but deemed it wiser not to ask. She had a feeling that the answer might not be one that she would want to hear. She took her own plate to the table and sat down. She was just about to pick up her knife and fork when she felt a funny sensation in her stomach and gasped.

'Are you all right?' Ben asked in concern.

'Yes.' She laughed when she felt it happening again. 'I think I just felt the baby move!'

'Really? What did it feel like?' he demanded eagerly.

'A sort of fluttering sensation...or maybe a tickly feeling.' She shook her head. 'It's difficult to describe.'

'I can't imagine how it must feel,' he admitted, starting to eat again.

'I don't suppose you can.' She put some salad onto her

plate and sighed. 'That was one of the things that Jo felt saddest about missing out on—feeling the baby moving around inside her.'

'But at least she had the joy of knowing that there was going to be a baby,' he said firmly.

'Yes, of course.' She looked down at her plate, wondering how he always knew what to say. Ben had the knack of coming out with just the right words when she needed to hear them most of all. It was very strange.

'What? Why are you frowning like that?' He put down his knife and fork then reached across the table and took hold of her hand. 'Come on, Anna, tell me. If something is worrying you, I want to know what it is.'

'I was just wondering how you always seem to know exactly the right thing to say,' she confessed softly.

'It isn't difficult when you care about someone as much as I care about you.'

The words seemed to hang in the air between them. Anna knew that he was waiting for her to say something but she didn't know how to respond. Should she admit that she cared about him, too, or would that be a stupid thing to do? Surely it would be better to laugh it off with some light remark, to turn away from the moment of truth rather than confront it?

She bit her lip in a quandary of indecision and heard him sigh. 'I realise that you don't want to hear me say things like that, Anna—'

'No!' The word seemed to explode from her of its own volition because she certainly hadn't planned on saying it. She took a deep breath, but it was as though she no longer had control of herself or her emotions. 'It…it means a lot to me to…to know how you feel.'

An expression of intense joy crossed his face as he pushed back his chair and stood up. Anna knew that she should call a halt while she had the chance, but she simply didn't have enough control left to do that. Ben came round the table and drew her to her feet, and his eyes seemed to blaze as they locked with hers.

'I'm crazy about you, Anna. You must know that. I love—'

'No! Please, don't! Don't say any more.' She pressed her fingers to his lips, shocked out of her inertia by a desperate need not to hear him say the words out loud. Maybe it was silly but if he didn't actually say that he loved her then she could deal with the situation somehow. 'It isn't right, Ben. Can't you see that?'

'No, I can't. How can I when it feels very right to me?'

He kissed her fingers, one by one, then gently lowered her hand to her side and held it there. 'But if you don't want me to say any more, I won't. It doesn't stop how I feel, of course. Nothing can alter that.'

She felt tears welling into her eyes when she heard the throbbing note in his voice. 'Oh, Ben, I never wanted this to happen...' she began brokenly.

'Shh. If I don't need to say anything, neither do you, sweetheart.' His expression was tender. 'I understand how you feel, Anna. Really I do. You don't have to explain anything to me.'

He drew her into his arms then and his mouth was so gentle when it found hers that she couldn't find it in her heart to fight what was happening. She lifted her face towards him, shuddering when the first tender assault on her senses turned in the blink of an eye to something far more intense. There was a new hunger about the way Ben's lips claimed hers now, an urgency to the way he drew her closer so that her body was pressed against the length of his.

Anna gasped when she felt the physical evidence of his desire yet it wasn't shock that she felt but a deep, burning need to respond. Ben wanted her and she—well, she wanted him just as much!

He drew back abruptly and his eyes seemed to burn as he stared at her. 'I want to make love to you, Anna. You know that, don't you?'

'Yes.' Her voice was little more than a whisper, the husky sound of it sending a shiver pulsing through him, and she felt his hands contract on her arms.

'It won't harm the baby if we make love, but it's your decision. I would never, ever do anything to hurt you.' He smoothed his hand almost reverently down her body, following the full swell of her breasts, the curve of her belly, and this time it was she who shivered because the sensations his touch had aroused shocked her so much.

Her eyes rose to his and she saw the understanding on his face even before she had tried to explain. 'I never expected...never thought...'

'That you would want to make love while you were pregnant?' His lips were tender as they skimmed up her cheek, his voice vibrating with a desire which he made no attempt to hide. Anna shivered again when she heard the passion that coated each word.

'Yes,' she admitted shakily, unable to lie.

'There are no rules in a situation like this, Anna,' he whispered, dropping butterfly-soft kisses across the bridge of her nose. 'So that means that we aren't breaking any.' He kissed her upper lip, then her bottom one, gently drawing it into his mouth, sighing when he heard her gasp. When his hands slid down her body again, she moaned out loud, unable to hide how the caress made her feel.

Ben responded by drawing her even closer, his hand splayed at the small of her back as he held her against him and let the urgent throbbing of his body show her very graphically how he felt. 'And there's nobody in the world who can tell us that what we're doing is wrong.'

His mouth found hers again and she was lost the very instant she felt his lips closing over hers. She opened her mouth for him then, feeling the heady rush of pleasure that filled her as his tongue sought entry and mated with hers in a ritual as old as time, yet one that felt so new and fresh to her that it seemed to arouse all her senses.

She clung to him as her legs threatened to give way, feeling the heat of his body flowing into hers, smelling the raw, male scent of him, tasting the passion they were creating together. When Ben swept her into his arms and carried her from the kitchen, she didn't protest. Her head was no longer in control. It was her heart that was in charge now, her heart that was dictating what happened next, and she didn't have the strength or the will-power to fight it.

Ben set her down in the middle of the bedroom and just looked at her. 'I thought you looked lovely the first time you wore that dress, but you look even more beautiful to-night.'

He kissed her gently then slowly reached behind her and slid the zipper down. With infinite care he slipped the dress off her shoulders and let it fall to the floor.

Anna stepped out of the pool of cloth, shivering when she saw the way he was looking at her as she stood there in the coffee-coloured silk slip that she wore beneath. Would he still find her attractive when she was completely undressed and he could see how the baby had made her body swell? The thought that he might be repulsed by how she looked made her heart turn over, but there was no time to reconsider what she was doing when he suddenly smiled at her.

'Now your turn. How are you with buttons?' He took

old of her hands and placed them on his chest, smiling encouragement when she hesitated.

Anna bit her lip as she started to unbutton his shirt. She was trembling so hard now that it seemed to take for ever to accomplish the simple task. However, Ben was patient to a fault, standing rock-still in front of her until she had undone the very last one.

He shrugged off the shirt and tossed it into the corner then turned to her again. 'My turn next.'

He slipped his fingers beneath the straps of her slip and slid them down her arms, then bent so that he could draw it off her body. Anna steadied herself by holding onto his shoulder as she stepped out of the silky fabric, feeling little flurries of alarm darting through her. All she had on now were a rather utilitarian bra and a pair of matching briefs, and she was suddenly overwhelmingly conscious of how she must look. She didn't think that she could bear it if Ben thought that she was ugly!

'You're beautiful, Anna, so very beautiful.'

There was a reverence in his voice as he straightened and looked at her that made her fears instantly evaporate. There wasn't a shred of doubt in her mind that he was telling her the truth. When he reached behind her and unclipped her bra she no longer felt ashamed or scared. She stood in front of him proudly, watching the desire that crossed his face as he cupped her breasts in his hands and lifted them so that he could place his mouth to her nipples.

Anna cried out when she felt the needle-sharp sensations shooting through her as he suckled her breasts. She had to grip his arms for support because the feeling was so intense that she could barely stand it.

Ben raised his head and she could see the passion that had turned his eyes almost black when he looked at her.

'This is what you want, isn't it, Anna? Tell me to stop if you still have doubts.'

She moistened her lips, feeling the pulsing hunger building deep inside her as he stroked her wet nipples with the pads of his thumbs. 'I don't want you to stop, Ben,' she admitted hoarsely. 'I want you to make love to me.'

'No woman will ever be loved as I am going to love you,' he bit out, bending to lift her into his arms. He carried her to the bed and laid her down on it, his expression saying all that needed to be said as he looked at her for a long moment after he had stripped off her briefs and she was lying naked in front of him.

Anna took hold of his hand and laid it on her stomach, pressing it gently against the swollen hardness. 'Love me, Ben,' she whispered. 'Please.'

It was all the invitation he needed. He quickly stripped off the rest of his clothes and lay down beside her, gathering her into his arms and holding her close so that she was in no doubt that it was what he wanted as well.

Anna closed her eyes, letting herself drift as passion claimed them, letting her heart have its way and her head be silenced. Maybe this was wrong and she would regret it, but she couldn't bear to stop what was happening. She couldn't bear to deny herself this time in Ben's arms even if it was a mistake!

CHAPTER NINE

MOONLIGHT streamed through the window, casting a silvery light over the room. Anna lay on her side, watching Ben as he slept. His skin was dappled with light, lending him a strangely ethereal appearance which was totally at odds with the flesh-and-blood man lying beside her. They had made love with a passion and intensity that made her heart race when she thought about it. It had been everything she could have dreamed of, which made it all the more difficult to know what to do.

Ben loved her. He hadn't said the words because she hadn't let him say them, but that didn't alter how he felt. How did she feel about him? It was a question which she had shied away from answering but she had to be honest with herself at last.

She loved him, too. She could never have *made* love with him if she hadn't loved him with all her heart. However, the situation wasn't straightforward. It wasn't simply a question of seeking the right answers then knowing what to do. There were too many other things to be taken into account.

She sighed as she rolled over and stared at the ceiling. How could she let Ben become involved in her life when it would mean such drastic changes for him? Maybe he felt that he could accept the baby at the present time, but how could she be sure that he wouldn't change his mind in the future? The thought that he might one day come to resent this child she was carrying scared her.

'What are you thinking?'

His voice was soft and deep, filled with so much love that Anna felt her heart ache. She kept her gaze focused on the ceiling, not wanting him to see how confused she felt. She had to be strong now, make her head take charge and not listen to the clamouring of her heart, but she couldn't do that if she let Ben persuade her that everything would work out.

'Nothing,' she replied woodenly.

'You'd be no good at poker, Anna Clemence.' He slid his arm around her and gently drew her onto her side so that she was forced to look at him. 'You're a rotten liar.'

She sighed. 'Is that a fact?'

'Yes.' He kissed her quickly on the mouth. 'I know for certain that you're lying there worrying your beautiful head about this situation, so there's no point pretending.' He framed her face between his hands and his gaze was fierce all of a sudden. 'There's nothing to worry about, Anna. I promise you!'

'I wish I could believe you,' she began shakily.

'Then let me convince you.'

His mouth was urgent this time, his hunger barely contained despite the hours they had spent already making love. Anna knew it was the wrong thing to do but she responded blindly as he made love to her again with a tenderness and passion that touched her soul. That Ben loved her this much was almost more than she could bear in the circumstances, but she couldn't deny his feelings any more than she could deny her own. She loved him with all her heart, with every scrap of her being, but sometimes love wasn't enough to guarantee that nobody would get hurt.

He gave her one last, achingly tender kiss then tossed back the quilt. 'I'm going to take a shower. It's time that we got a few things straight and I won't be able to keep my mind on what needs to be said if I stay here.'

'Ben, I—'

'No.' He shook his head. 'Don't say anything now. We need to sit down and discuss this calmly, rationally, Anna. I know I'm going to have a job convincing you that what we have is too important to risk losing, and I don't want us to make any mistakes.'

Anna sighed as he left the bedroom. He must have guessed how uncertain she was, but how could she allow herself to be persuaded when in her heart she knew that it would be wrong? She wanted to do what was right for all of them and letting herself be carried away by her feelings for Ben—and his for her—wasn't the way.

There was a heaviness in her heart as she got up and slipped on a robe. When Ben had finished in the bathroom she took a shower then got dressed even though it was gone midnight, needing the protection of clothes to give her the illusion that she was in control. However, as she left the bedroom she knew that was all it was—an illusion. She didn't feel in control of anything at that moment!

'I've made some tea. I thought it might be better than coffee at this time of the night.'

Ben got up as she went into the sitting room and poured her a cup of tea. He placed it on the table in front of the sofa but Anna chose to sit in a chair instead. It would be difficult enough to keep a clear head when she had to face him, but impossible if she sat next to him.

'Do you want to go first or shall I?' There was an edge in his voice which she had never heard in it before, and she looked sharply at him. He wasn't looking at her but she could tell from the taut line of his jaw that he was steeling himself for what was about to happen.

'You may as well start,' she said softly, wishing that there was a way to make this easier for both of them.

'Very well, then. I love you, Anna.' He shook his head

when she went to protest. 'No. There's no point in lying about how I feel. I love you and I'm not ashamed of the fact. I believe that we could have a future together but I sense that you don't agree. I think that you've got some crazy idea into your head that the baby is a handicap.'

'It isn't crazy at all. The truth is that this baby isn't your responsibility, Ben. It wouldn't be fair to turn your life upside down by expecting you to take care of it.'

'You wouldn't be turning my life upside down! You'd be giving me the chance to do something that I want to do!'

He stood up abruptly and paced across the room then swung round. 'I *want* to be part of this baby's life, Anna. I *need* to be a part of yours! Don't deny me either of those things, I beg you!'

She shook her head in despair, hating to hear him sound so distraught. 'It isn't that simple! All right, so maybe you feel that you can love this child now, but how about in the future? Can you guarantee that you'll still feel the same and that you won't come to resent having to look after it? What happens if we have children of our own—would you be able to love this child as much as you would love them?'

'Of course I would! I can't believe that you're asking me a question like that.' His face was set as he came back across the room and stood in front of her. 'I shall love this child every bit as much as any other children that we might have. Why on earth would you doubt it?'

Anna looked away, not wanting to see the hurt and anger in his eyes. She didn't doubt that he believed what he said, but she couldn't dismiss what her brother-in-law had told her, that no man really wanted another man's child. Perhaps if the baby had been half hers then she would have felt easier about the idea, but it was Jo's and Mike's child.

The reality was that Ben would be committing himself

to caring for a child that wasn't even *hers*, let alone his! How could he not come to resent the responsibility that had been thrust upon him? She didn't think she could bear it if a time came when he regretted having fallen in love with her.

She was still trying to find a way to explain all that to him when he spoke, and she shivered when she heard the unaccustomed harshness in his voice. 'Maybe this hasn't anything to do with the baby at all. Perhaps the real truth is that you have doubts about your own feelings, Anna. It could be that I was presuming too much to think that you loved me.'

Anna bit her lip. The urge to confess that she loved him with all her heart was almost too great to bear. However, if she did that then he would find a way to convince her that her fears were groundless. Was she really prepared to risk ruining his life because, selfishly, she couldn't bear to live the rest of hers without him?

Her head spun with all the thoughts that were whirling inside it but she simply couldn't decide what to do for the best. And in the end Ben took her silence as his answer. 'It seems that I owe you an apology, Anna. Obviously, I completely misjudged the situation. All I can say is that you can rest assured that this will be the end of it.'

He didn't say anything else before he left the room. Anna heard him walking into the kitchen then the sound of the back door opening and closing. She sat right where she was, recalling the day when she had first met Ben. Then she had stood on the stairs after he had left, listening to the silence. She had felt so alone that day, so bereft, yet it had been nothing compared to how she felt at that moment. This time it felt as though Ben had taken her heart away with him when he had walked out of the door.

* * *

'Lucy is being discharged this afternoon. I thought I'd drive over to the hospital to collect her if you wouldn't mind covering for me.'

Anna was in Adam's room, discussing a patient's treatment, when Ben knocked on the door. It was almost a week since the night they had slept together and he had treated her with faultless courtesy ever since. It was obvious that he intended to stick to his promise never to raise the subject of how he felt about her, and although she knew that she should be relieved, it still hurt to have him treat her so distantly all the time.

'Of course. What's going to happen about her? I don't like the idea of her being stuck in that poky little bedsit again when she comes home,' Adam asked, frowning.

'Janice Robertson has invited Lucy to stay with her for a couple of weeks.' Ben shrugged. 'I'm hoping to persuade Lucy that it would be a good idea, but she didn't seem keen when I mentioned it to her. She said that she didn't like accepting favours from people.'

Anna frowned. She couldn't help noticing how weary he sounded that day. Her heart twisted painfully when she saw the lines of strain that bracketed his mouth. It was obvious that the situation between them was taking its toll on him and she couldn't help feeling guilty, even though she knew that she had made the right decision.

'Try and talk her round to the idea,' Adam advised him. 'The last thing we want is a repeat of what happened. Did you find out why Lucy took that overdose, by the way?'

'It appears that she'd had a final demand for her water bill. She simply didn't have the money to pay it and was scared stiff because they were threatening to cut off her water supply,' Ben said grimly. 'I've been onto the water company and told them in no uncertain terms what I think about their methods. They've promised to look into the situation and not send her any more demands.'

'Good. It comes to something when people are driven to taking their own lives because they can't afford the basic necessities,' Adam said disgustedly.

Anna shivered. She was very aware that she, too, would be forced to live off a pittance soon. She couldn't help wondering how she was going to manage after the baby was born.

She quickly excused herself, not wanting Ben to suspect what was going through her mind. It wouldn't be fair to add to his burden by letting him see how worried she was. She had made her decision to go it alone and it had been the right thing to do. She would just have to take each day as it came.

Fortunately, her next patient arrived soon afterwards so Anna was able to set aside her own problems while she concentrated on work. Edna Johnson had been receiving treatment for a leg ulcer for some time and it was obvious that she was concerned about why it wouldn't seem to heal.

'I don't know why it hasn't cleared up, do you, dear?' Edna asked. 'I've been very careful not to knock it or damage it in any way.'

'Ulcers are notoriously difficult to treat,' Anna explained, removing the old dressing so that she could examine the open sore. The floor of the ulcer was bright red whilst the surrounding tissue had a thin blue line running around its edge, marking the area where new cells were growing. She was pleased to see that it looked a lot better than it had done the last time she'd seen it, and said so.

'It looks much better today, anyway. Those wet dressings that I put on have helped enormously.'

'I still don't understand why I got it in the first place. I only banged my leg on the coffee-table and I must have done that dozens of times over the years,' Edna declared.

'I'm afraid it's something that tends to happen when you're getting older,' Anna explained, carefully cleaning the ulcer. 'Your circulation probably isn't as good as it used to be, which means that there's less blood getting to the site of the infection. It makes it that more difficult for any damaged areas to heal.'

'It's no fun, getting old,' Edna observed wryly. 'If it isn't one thing it's another. Inside I still feel twenty-five but outside I'm falling to bits!'

'Nonsense!' Anna laughed. 'I hope I look as good as you do when I'm your age. Didn't you tell me that you'd just had your eightieth birthday the last time I saw you?'

'That's right.' Edna laughed as well. 'I never thought I'd reach this age and that's for sure. It makes me even more determined to get the last bit of pleasure out of each day because I haven't got that many left.' She glanced at her leg. 'I'm certainly not letting a little thing like that deter me from having fun!'

'Good for you.' Anna finished applying the fresh dressing then helped the old lady pull up her stocking. 'That should do for another week. Make an appointment on your way out and I'll see you next week.'

'How long will you be working here now, dear?' Edna asked as Anna walked her to the door. 'I'm knitting a little coat and bootees for your baby and I wanted to know how long I'd have to get them finished. My fingers aren't as nimble as they used to be so it takes me that bit more time.'

'Why, that's very kind of you!' Anna exclaimed, deeply touched by the old lady's kindness. 'I'm here for several weeks yet.'

'Oh, that's fine,' Edna said. 'I'll see you next week, then.'

Anna sighed as the old lady left. She hadn't expected the patients to take any interest in her baby but several of them had asked her when it was due. It struck her how much she was going to miss working at the surgery. Maybe she should think about taking Adam up on his offer of a part-time post after the baby was born. It would solve a number of problems if she knew that she had a job to come back to.

She glanced round as Ben's door opened, feeling her heart start to ache when she heard his voice. Just the sound of it made her want to rush into his room and throw her arms around him, but that wouldn't be fair. She couldn't switch on and off like that—one minute making him think that she wanted him and the next minute rejecting him. She either had a future with Ben or she didn't, and she had made her decision.

The time flew past so that before Anna knew it there was just a week of her contract left to work. Over seven months pregnant now, her body had undergone a lot of changes so that sometimes she got a real shock when she caught sight of herself in the mirror.

She had registered with a practice in a neighbouring town for her antenatal care, and regular check-ups had reassured her that the baby was fit and healthy. After her last check-up she had visited an estate agent's office in the town and asked them to send her details of any flats that became available in the area. Adam had told her that she could stay on in the flat over the surgery for however long she wanted to, but she wanted to find somewhere else to live as quickly as possible. Frankly, it would be too stressful to continue seeing Ben on a daily basis.

As for Ben, he had continued to behave impeccably towards her. He was polite, courteous and supportive whenever she needed his professional help. However, she was very much aware how much effort it cost him to behave that way. She hated the thought that she was hurting him yet she felt powerless to do anything about it.

She tried to console herself with the thought that one day he would meet someone else, but the idea of him loving another woman was very painful. She loved him, she wanted him, but she *wouldn't* do anything that might ultimately hurt him or the baby!

Eileen and Hilary had organised a farewell party for her, brushing aside her objections that she didn't want any fuss. It was arranged for the Friday night, her last day at work, and it was to be held in the surgery after closing time. Beth had been invited and was bringing Hannah with her, and Eileen was bringing her husband Ron.

When the day finally arrived, Anna was touched to receive cards and presents from a number of patients. Harold Newcombe and his wife came in specially to bring her a card and a fluffy, yellow teddy bear to put in the baby's crib. They had only just left when Edna Johnson arrived and Anna was struck almost speechless when she opened the tissue-wrapped parcel and saw the cobweb-fine matinee coat and matching bootees the old lady had made for her.

'They are really beautiful, Mrs Johnson. I don't think I've ever seen such delicate work,' she said truthfully.

'I'm so glad you like them, dear. I must admit that I enjoyed making them.' Edna smiled ruefully. 'My grandchildren are in their teens now so they're not all that keen on Granny's knitting. I don't think it's trendy enough!'

Anna laughed. 'Well, my baby is going to look beautiful in this lovely little outfit. He or she will be proud to wear it.'

She glanced round when she heard footsteps behind her, feeling her heart starting to drum when she saw Ben. He stopped when he reached them and looked at the lacy little jacket she was holding.

'Is that for the baby?' he asked quietly. 'It's beautiful.'

'It is.' It was an effort to behave naturally but Anna knew that it would be unforgivable to let him see the tumult she was feeling. Just having him standing beside her seemed to have made her blood heat an extra degree or two and her heart pound. When he reached over and took one of the bootees out of the tissue paper and his hand brushed hers, she drew in a sharp breath.

Had Ben felt it too? she wondered. Had he felt the lightning-fast dart of awareness that had sparked between them?

'They're so tiny, aren't they?' he said roughly, his voice throbbing in a way that immediately answered her question. 'It's hard to imagine any feet being small enough to fit into them.'

'Oh, they'll soon grow, believe me.' Edna patted her arm. 'You make sure that you enjoy every minute because before you know it your little one will be walking and talking!'

'I'll bear it in mind,' Anna replied, forcing a smile. She was achingly conscious of Ben standing beside her as she and Edna exchanged a few more pleasantries before the old lady left.

'It was kind of her to make these for me, wasn't it?' she said stiltedly, making a great production of rewrapping the tiny garments.

'It was. Eileen said that several patients popped in this morning with cards and presents.' He smiled but she saw the pain that lay deep in his eyes. 'Everyone is sorry that you're leaving, Anna. People here have grown very fond of you.'

'I've grown very fond of them, too,' she admitted softly. She took a deep breath but it didn't ease the sudden constriction in her lungs. They might be having a conversation about the people in the town but she knew that on a different level Ben was telling her that his feelings for her hadn't changed.

It almost broke her heart not to be able to tell him the truth about how she felt, but that wouldn't have been fair. Ben would have found it even harder to accept her decision not to let him play a part in her future if she admitted that she loved him. It was an effort to keep her tone light when she knew how much she must be hurting him. 'Still, I'm sure that they'll soon forget about me once Beth comes back.'

'Maybe.'

He gave her a strained smile then carried on along the corridor. Anna went back to her room, and for the rest of the morning she refused to let herself think about anything other than work. There would be time to think about everything else after the day had ended—too much time, in fact. She would have a whole lifetime to think about Ben and what might have happened if the situation had been different.

Anna had decided to wear the blue dress again that night for the party. She went up to the flat as soon as they had shut the surgery and quickly changed. Eileen and Hilary were downstairs, putting the finishing touches to the buffet, and Beth and Hannah were due to arrive at any time. Bearing in mind all the trouble everyone had gone to, the least she could do was to be there to greet them, even though the last thing she felt like doing was celebrating. Leaving work meant leaving Ben, and that wasn't something she was looking forward to.

Adam was opening a bottle of champagne when she went downstairs. He greeted her with a smile, although she couldn't help noticing the rather troubled expression on his face. However, before she could ask him if there was anything wrong he held up the bottle.

'How about a glass of champagne? I don't think one glass will do you or the baby any harm.' He handed her a glass then looked round as Eileen and Hilary appeared. 'Champagne, ladies?'

'Oh, lovely!' Eileen declared, happily accepting a glass. Both receptionists had taken the time to change and they looked very smart. Anna appreciated the effort they had put into making the party a success and only wished that she felt more like enjoying it. However, the thought of not seeing Ben again once she had left Winton was like a black cloud hanging over her.

Adam had just poured himself a glass of the wine when there was a knock on the door. He went away to answer it, coming back a few minutes later with Beth and Hannah, as well as Eileen's husband who had arrived at the same time. He dispensed more glasses, although Hannah's contained sparkling apple juice rather than champagne. How difficult it was going to be to get on with her life when there were all these constant reminders of him.

Anna felt a little stab of pain pierce her heart as she recalled the night she had cooked supper for Ben and he had suggested that they pretend the apple juice was champagne.

Beth brought Hannah over to speak to her once they had their drinks. Anna did her best to respond as the other woman chatted away but she was having difficulty concentrating. There was still no sign of Ben and she couldn't help wondering where he had got to. She frowned when Adam called for order. Surely he wasn't going to make a start without waiting for Ben?

'I don't intend to waste too much time by making a

speech, you'll be glad to hear. However, I'm sure that you would all like to join me in drinking a toast to Anna, and wishing her well for the future,' Adam began, only to have Beth interrupt him.

'Just a minute, darling. You've forgotten Ben. Is he still in his room? I'll go and fetch him.'

'Ben couldn't stay for the party, I'm afraid,' Adam informed her tersely. 'He had something urgent to do. He asked me to make his apologies to you all.'

Anna stared at her glass as Adam carried on with the toast. She could feel her eyes burning with tears and was terrified that everyone would see that she was upset. Ben hadn't wanted to stay for the party because he hadn't been able to face the thought of her leaving. It almost broke her heart to imagine the anguish he must be going through.

'What's going on, Anna? Have you and Ben had some sort of a disagreement?'

She looked up when Beth touched her on the arm. She could see the compassion on the other woman's face and all of a sudden the tears started to roll down her cheeks. 'It's a bit more complicated than that,' she whispered brokenly.

Beth quickly steered her into a corner so that the others couldn't see what was happening. 'Do you want to talk about it?'

'Not really. There's no point because it won't help.' She found a tissue in her pocket and quickly dried her eyes. 'I'm sorry. I didn't mean to spoil the evening for you. I'm fine now, really.'

Beth looked sceptical. 'You don't look fine to me. Look, Anna, I hate to see you upset like this. If there's anything at all that I can do…'

'There isn't,' Anna said quickly. 'I appreciate your kindness, Beth, but there isn't anything that you or anyone else can do, believe me.'

'Has it something to do with the baby?' Beth asked astutely. She sighed when Anna nodded. 'I thought so. I know it can't be easy for you and Ben to work this out. It's a difficult situation and nobody can really tell you how to deal with it, but I hope that you'll believe me when I say that if you love someone enough, there's always a solution to even the biggest problem.'

She glanced across the room at Adam and Anna saw an expression of love cross her face. 'You just need to follow what your heart is telling you to do, even though sometimes it takes a great deal of courage.'

She didn't say anything else, switching the subject to something far less personal. Anna responded as best she could as Eileen came to join them but she was only half listening. Was Beth right? she wondered. Should she have listened to her heart and not to her head? Was she in danger of throwing away something so precious, so special, because she lacked courage?

Her mind spun all evening long so that she was both physically and mentally exhausted with the effort of trying to hide how she felt from everyone else. It was a relief when Adam announced that it was time that he and Beth took Hannah home. The others quickly followed suit, kissing Anna and offering her their best wishes before they left.

She went up to the flat after everyone had gone and sat for a long time, just thinking about what Beth had said to her. She wanted to believe that it was true, desperately wanted to find the courage to follow her heart, but there was a tiny bit of her that was still urging caution. If she made a mistake, it wouldn't be just her who got hurt.

In the end she went to bed because she was worn out with the effort of trying to sort out the muddle inside her head. She'd had trouble sleeping lately because the baby seemed to grow more active the moment she lay down. However, that night she fell into a deep sleep almost as soon as her head touched the pillow. She was awakened some time later by the sound of the telephone ringing.

She struggled out of bed, feeling groggy and disorientated as she wondered who could be calling her at that time of the night.

Unless it was Ben?

Her heart started to pound. All of a sudden she didn't know what she was going to say to him. Should she tell him that she was starting to have doubts about whether she had made the right decision? Did she have the courage and conviction to follow her heart?

Her hand was shaking so hard that she could barely hold the receiver to her ear. It took her a moment to recognise the voice on the other end of the line, and several more to follow what Adam was telling her. She felt a wave of sickness hit her as it finally sank in.

Ben had been involved in a car accident. He was in hospital and the doctors weren't sure if he would live.

CHAPTER TEN

'THE next few hours will be critical. We've done everything we can but Dr Cole has lost a lot of blood.'

The surgeon sighed as he pulled off his cap. He had come straight from Theatre to speak to them and he was still wearing a green scrub suit. 'Shock is our biggest problem at the moment. We have removed his spleen and stopped the bleeding but it could go either way, I'm afraid.'

'They told us in A and E that there might be some spinal damage,' Adam said tersely. 'How soon will you know for certain?'

'It could be some time yet,' the surgeon explained. 'There's severe swelling around the lumbar region so the X-rays we've taken aren't conclusive. We'll need to redo them and do a CAT scan as well before we know for certain if any damage has been done to the spinal cord.'

Anna turned away as Adam asked the man another question. Maybe it was cowardly but she simply couldn't take hearing anything more. The past few hours had been a nightmare. After Adam had collected her from the flat they had driven straight to the hospital. Ben had been taken by ambulance to the A and E unit so they had gone there first and been shown into the relatives' room to wait for the doctor.

It had seemed like hours before the registrar had come to tell them that Ben had been taken to Theatre and that he would be transferred to the intensive care unit afterwards. Although the registrar hadn't said so, Anna had known that he'd been wondering if Ben would actually make it that far.

The details of the accident were sketchy but, from what little she had learned, it appeared that a lorry had jackknifed on the wet road and ploughed into Ben's car. According to a police officer who had attended the accident, he was lucky to be alive. However, there was no guarantee that he was going to live, as the surgeon had pointed out.

Leaving the two men talking, she went out to the corridor and made her way to the IC unit. She paused in the doorway, letting her eyes adjust to the dim lighting. There were six beds in the ward and Ben had been placed in the one nearest to the door. He'd been attached to an array of different monitors and machinery after he'd been brought down from Theatre. His heart rate, blood pressure, breathing and oxygen levels were being constantly assessed. One drip was replacing the blood and fluids that he had lost, another was keeping him sedated and free from pain. Everything humanly and technically possible was being done to keep him alive, but would it be enough?

'Come back and sit down. You won't do yourself or Ben any good by tiring yourself out.'

Adam gently led her back to the waiting room and sat her down in a chair. His face was stern as he sat down beside her. 'He's going to make it, Anna. He's young and fit and that counts for a lot in a situation like this.'

'How can you be sure? You heard what the surgeon said, that the next few hours will be critical. I don't think I could bear it if he died!'

She couldn't go on as the fear rose inside her. Adam sighed as he put his arm around her shoulders. 'He isn't going to die! You mustn't think like that. You've got to be positive and believe that he'll pull through.'

He sounded so certain that she looked at him curiously.
'I think you really believe that.'

'I do. When Hannah was desperately ill Beth told me
that I had to believe that she would get better. I know it
isn't very scientific but I honestly and truly believe that it
helped.' He smiled at her. 'So don't ever underestimate the
power of positive thought, Anna. Keep willing Ben to get
better.'

'I shall,' she whispered. She took a deep breath then got
up and went back to the unit, unable to rest until she knew
how Ben was doing. There was a nurse checking his drips
and she smiled when she saw Anna standing by the door.
She finished what she was doing then came to speak to her.

'Would you like to sit with Dr Cole?' she suggested. She
frowned as Adam came to join them. 'I'm afraid there's
only room for one of you. We can't have too many visitors
around a bed, you understand.'

'I'll wait here,' Adam offered immediately. 'You go and
sit with him, Anna.'

'Are you sure?' she queried.

'Quite sure.' He glanced at his watch and grimaced. 'I'd
better go and phone Beth. She'll be worried sick if she
doesn't hear from me soon.'

Anna followed the nurse into the ward as he hurried
away. She smiled her thanks as the other woman drew up
a chair beside the bed for her to sit on.

'You can hold his hand if you want to,' the nurse told
her softly. It was very quiet in the ward with only the click-
ing and humming of the machinery. All the patients in there
were seriously ill and needed peace and quiet as well as
skilled nursing care. 'He's heavily sedated so don't worry
if he doesn't respond. However, in my experience, patients
often know when there's someone sitting with them.'

She looked round as a monitor began to bleep then

turned back to Anna and smiled reassuringly when one of the other nurses hurried to attend to it. 'I know how scary it is, seeing him like this, but if we can get him over the next few hours then he stands a good chance. You hold his hand and let him know that you're here.' She glanced at Anna's tummy. 'Let him know that you're *both* here. It's the best medicine in the world, believe me.'

Anna sighed as the nurse moved away. It was obvious that the other woman believed that the baby was Ben's.

If only it was his child, she thought wistfully, none of this would have happened. Ben wouldn't have been driving along that road tonight and that lorry wouldn't have hit him. They would have been together at the party, enjoying spending time with their friends and looking forward to the future. How bitterly ironic that her attempts to save him from getting hurt had ended like this.

It was pointless dwelling on it, however, so she tried to put it out of her mind as she took hold of his hand. His skin felt unusually cool to the touch but she could feel his pulse tapping away and it was reassuring to feel it. She found herself wondering if the nurse had been right and if he knew that she was there at his bedside. If so, she hoped that he could feel her willing him to get better. She needed him too much to lose him!

The night crawled past and Anna soon lost track of time. Staff came and went at intervals, checking monitors and changing drips. There were no windows in the intensive care unit so it wasn't until one of the nurses brought her a message from Adam to say that he'd had to leave to go back to Winton for surgery that she realised it must be morning.

She stayed where she was, uncaring that her body was stiff and cramped from sitting in the hard chair. If she had to stay there for a week, a month or a year even, she would do so! It didn't matter how long it took if there was a chance that it might help Ben get better.

She must have dozed off eventually because she woke with a start when one of the nurses tapped her on the shoulder and told her that she would have to leave while the consultant did his rounds. She got up unsteadily, feeling strangely disorientated as she left the hushed atmosphere of the IC unit and was suddenly assailed by the hustle and bustle of the busy hospital. She wasn't sure what to do with herself until it was time to go back and sit with Ben.

'There you are! I was just going to see if I could find someone to fetch you. What you need is something to eat and drink. Come along.'

Anna blinked as Beth suddenly appeared at her side. 'What are you doing here?' she asked in confusion.

'Making sure that you don't make yourself ill,' Beth told her firmly, taking hold of her arm and steering her toward the lifts.

'Oh, but I can't leave,' she protested, hanging back.

'You can and you will.' Beth stopped and glared at her. 'Do you know how long you've been sitting by that bed? No? Well, from my reckoning it must be at least eight hours. You need to take a break, Anna.'

She shook her head. 'I'm fine, really I am—' she began, but Beth didn't give her time to finish.

'If you won't think about yourself then think about the baby. Ben will be furious when he finds out that you wouldn't take even a few minutes' break.'

Anna felt her throat close up. 'You don't understand. I'm afraid to leave in case something happens to him. I want to be here with him, Beth. I *need* to be here! It's the only thing I can do that might help him.'

'I do understand,' Beth said gently. 'I'd feel the same if it was Adam lying in that bed. But you're not helping Ben by making yourself ill. Just take a few minutes to have something to eat then you can come back and sit with him again. Please.'

Anna hesitated but she could see the sense in what her friend was saying. 'All right, then,' she conceded reluctantly. 'But just ten minutes. I don't want to be away any longer than that.'

'Ten minutes it is,' Beth assured her, summoning the lift. 'We'll go to the coffee-shop in the foyer. The service there is usually pretty quick. You'll be back here in no time, trust me.'

It didn't take them long to reach the coffee-shop on the ground floor. There were few people in there at that time of the day. It was too early for normal visiting hours so there were only a handful of people scattered about the room.

Beth pointed to a table in the corner. 'Let's sit over there where it's quiet. What do you want to drink, tea or coffee? And how about something to eat?'

'Tea, please, and nothing to eat.' She grimaced. 'I feel a bit sick, actually.'

Beth sighed as she took a tray from the rack by the door. 'No wonder, after the night you've had. Anyway, go and sit down while I fetch the drinks.'

Anna made her way across the room and sat down, feeling waves of exhaustion washing over her. The long night had taken its toll but she was determined to return to Ben's bedside as soon as she could. Even now he might be wondering where she was, thinking that she hadn't cared enough to stay with him.

A sob caught in her throat and she pressed a hand to her mouth. Why hadn't she told him how she really felt about him when she'd had the chance? The thought that he might never know how much she loved him was more than she could bear.

'Here you are. I got some toast as well. You might be able to manage a slice.' Beth put the tray on the table then looked at her in concern. 'Are you OK?'

'Not really,' Anna admitted huskily. 'I keep wondering what I'll do if Ben doesn't make it...'

She couldn't go on because it was too painful to think about it. Beth sighed as she sat down and poured them both a cup of tea. 'He's got this far, Anna. That's a good sign, you know it is.'

'Maybe, but he isn't out of danger yet. He lost an awful lot of blood and then there are the other injuries that he suffered.' She picked up the cup then had to put it back down because her hand was shaking too much to hold it. 'Did Adam tell you that he might have damaged his spine? We won't know for certain until he has more X-rays and a scan because there's so much localised swelling.'

'Let's not look on the black side,' Beth said firmly. 'His spine might just be bruised. You know as well as I do that heavy bruising causes massive swelling. Once it goes down he'll be fine.'

'I suppose so. And I suppose you're right about not looking on the black side. It's just that I feel so guilty,' she confessed brokenly.

'Why on earth should you feel guilty?' Beth demanded.

'Because if I hadn't let Ben think that I didn't...didn't care about him, this might never have happened.' She saw Beth looking at her and knew that she had to explain even though it was painful to talk about what had happened. 'Ben told me a few weeks ago that he loved me, you see. He tried to convince me that we had a future together.'

'Obviously, he didn't succeed. Why, Anna? Because you weren't sure how you felt about him at the time?'

She shook her head, wishing the answer were that simple. 'No. I knew that I was in love with him, too. I just thought it best if I didn't tell him how I felt. It seemed the right thing to do in the circumstances.'

'Because of the baby?' Beth suggested quietly.

'Yes. I was afraid that Ben might come to regret taking on the responsibility for this child,' she admitted huskily. 'I was terrified that he might grow to resent it in time. I couldn't bear to think that he might one day wish that he'd never met me.'

'Hogwash!' Beth declared, then grinned when Anna stared at her in surprise. 'Sorry to be so blunt, but I can't imagine where you got such a crazy idea like that.'

'From something my brother-in-law said to me.' She sighed as she picked up a spoon and stirred her tea. 'He warned me that no man would want to take on another man's child, and that if he did then he would end up regretting it. It's been at the back of my mind all along and I suppose that's why I was so afraid of making a mistake.'

'I expect some men couldn't handle the situation but Ben isn't one of them. He's like Adam in a lot of respects—rock solid and dependable, the kind of man on whom you can rely totally,' Beth said firmly. 'If Ben said that he wanted to spend his life with you and the baby then you can believe him, Anna. He isn't going to suddenly change his mind.'

'I think you're right,' Anna said wonderingly. It felt as though the veil of confusion had lifted all of a sudden so that her mind was crystal clear at last. Never mind what Mike had said, *she* knew that Ben had been telling her the truth! 'In fact, I'm *sure* you're right!'

'Then when Ben wakes up, make sure you tell him that,' Beth said resolutely, then laughed. 'And I shall expect an invitation to the wedding!'

'You'll be top of the list, I promise you!' Anna laughed as well, feeling the joy bubbling inside her. Maybe it was too soon to start making plans but as soon as Ben was feeling better she would tell him the truth about how she felt. All they needed now was for him to get better—and he would. He would!

She was in a far more positive frame of mind when she returned to the IC unit a short time later. When the ward sister called her into the office in the middle of the afternoon and explained that the consultant was so pleased with Ben's progress that they would gradually start to reduce his sedatives, she could have jumped for joy. The only cloud on the horizon was the fact that nobody knew for certain how bad his other injuries were. However, she was confident that whatever happened they could face it together. She loved him, she wanted to spend the rest of her life with him. There was no obstacle so big that they couldn't deal with it!

She went back to the ward and sat by his bed while she waited for him to wake up. He had been taken off the ventilator and was breathing on his own now. When she saw his eyelids starting to flicker a short time later she squeezed his hand, her heart overflowing with love when she felt the answering pressure of his fingers.

His eyes opened slowly and he looked round in confusion. She moved closer, bending over so that he could see her better, smiling when he finally focused on her face. 'Hi, there. How are you feeling?'

'Sore.' His voice rasped painfully and he swallowed. 'Throat hurts.'

'That's because of the tube. It will soon feel better.'

'Tube?' His gaze moved away from her and he frowned when he saw all the machinery. 'What happened? Where am I?'

'You were in an accident and you're in hospital. But you're going to be fine.'

'Accident,' he repeated uncertainly. He took a deep breath and she could tell that he was struggling to make sense of what she'd said. 'I remember now. There was this lorry and I couldn't get out of the way…'

He tailed off and she squeezed his hand. 'Try not to think about it. Just concentrate on getting better. You're doing great.'

'Am I?' He sighed wearily. 'I ache all over. The only parts of me that don't hurt are my legs.'

He stopped and she saw the shock that crossed his face. 'Why can't I feel my legs, Anna? What's wrong with them?'

She wasn't sure what to say. Would it be right to tell him the truth when it would be such a shock for him? He was still very weak and she was afraid that it might be too much for him to deal with at that moment. It was a relief when the sister suddenly appeared and asked Anna if she would mind leaving as the consultant was on his way back to have a word with Ben.

Ben didn't say anything when she told him that she would be back shortly. She wasn't sure if he even heard her. She bent and kissed him on the cheek, feeling her heart aching when she saw how he avoided her eyes. It was obvious that he was adding everything up and reaching his own conclusion, and she wished with all her heart that there was a way to reassure him. However, it would be wrong to make promises that she might not be able to keep.

She went back to the waiting room and spent the time pacing the floor, unable to sit down and relax as she wondered how Ben had taken the news. It seemed an age before the sister came to find her and she felt her heart sink when she saw the expression on the other woman's face. She had already half prepared herself for bad news before the sister asked her to sit down. But nothing could have prepared her for the message that the sister had for her—Ben had given strict instructions that he didn't want to see her again.

'I don't understand,' she whispered incredulously. 'You must have got it wrong. Why wouldn't he want to see me? I have to speak to him and sort this out...'

'I'm sorry but it's out of the question,' the sister said firmly, standing up and barring her way as Anna went to the door. 'Dr Cole was adamant that he didn't want you visiting him again. There's nothing I can do except follow his instructions, I'm afraid.'

No amount of pleading would make her change her mind. Anna left the hospital in a daze a short time later, unable to understand why Ben had made such a decision. It didn't make sense unless—unless he had realised all of a sudden that he didn't love her and had been too embarrassed to tell her to her face.

Anna felt her heart curl up inside her at the thought. She desperately didn't want to believe it, but it was a well-known fact that people often re-evaluated their lives straight after an accident.

Was that what Ben had done? she wondered sickly. Had he taken a long, hard look at his feelings and realised that he didn't love her? She had no idea, but it felt as though the bottom had fallen out of her world.

The next few days passed in a blur. Anna spent most of the time just sitting in the flat. She knew that Ben had been moved from the IC unit to the orthopaedic ward but he was still refusing to see her despite repeated phone calls to the hospital, begging him to reconsider. She was at her wits' end when Adam came to see her on the Wednesday after morning surgery had finished.

'I don't know what's going on, Anna, but you look dreadful,' he said bluntly when she let him in. He sighed as he studied her wan face and the inky shadows under her eyes. 'So does Ben, for that matter. What on earth is this all about? Why has he refused to see you? I can't get a word out of him so maybe you can throw some light on what's happened.'

'I don't know any more than you do,' she admitted, wrapping her arms around herself. She seemed to feel permanently cold of late, and even though she had turned on the heating in the flat she was shivering.

She led the way into the sitting room and sat down in front of the fire. 'I've phoned the hospital umpteen times, begging him to see me, but he keeps refusing. H-he's given strict instructions that I'm not allowed to visit him.'

Her voice caught and she heard Adam sigh. 'If he wasn't ill, I could happily shake some sense into him! All this nonsense isn't doing either him or you any good.'

She smiled sadly. 'I don't know if that makes me feel better or worse. I just feel even more confused, in fact. If Ben's upset, why is he being so pig-headed?'

'I've no idea.' Adam's tone was grim. 'I'll have a word with him tonight and see if I can talk some sense into him.'

'Would you?' she said eagerly. 'Better still, maybe I could come to the hospital with you, then I'd be there if he changes his mind.'

'I'm not sure that would be a good idea,' he began.

'Please, Adam! It's driving me mad sitting here, wondering why he won't see me.'

'All right, then, but only if you promise me that you'll try to rest.' He patted her shoulder as he got up to leave. 'We don't want another member of staff in hospital. It isn't good for our reputation!'

She laughed hollowly as she saw him out but she tried

to do as he'd said. She spent the afternoon lying on the sofa and felt a little better when it was time to get ready to go to the hospital.

She dressed with care, putting on the blue dress again and spending extra time on her make-up to disguise the damage the past few days had wrought. There was no guarantee that Ben would see her, of course, but if he did, she had made up her mind that she would tell him the truth. She would tell him how she felt about him and hope that it would help him realise that they had too much to lose.

Adam went into the ward on his own at first. He was gone for a long time and Anna was close to despair when he finally came back to tell her that Ben had agreed to see her.

She made her way down the ward, feeling her heart racing as she approached the bed. Ben was strapped to a spinal board, his head supported by a cradle that stopped him turning and possibly damaging his spine. He looked so pale and drawn that all she wanted to do was to hug him and tell him that she loved him, but he didn't give her the chance.

'I only agreed to see you tonight because Adam begged me to,' he said bluntly. 'But it isn't going to make any difference. I don't want you visiting me here again. Is that clear?'

Anna shivered when she heard the harshness in his voice. Frankly, she had difficulty believing that he would speak to her that way. She felt a little spurt of anger rise hotly inside her. Ben had made up his mind and he wouldn't even pay her the courtesy of discussing this situation!

'No, it isn't clear,' she shot back. 'I think I deserve to know what I've done wrong.'

'You haven't done anything wrong,' he said flatly, staring at the ceiling.

'Well, it certainly doesn't feel like that to me!' She moved closer to the bed so he couldn't avoid having to look at her. 'I think I deserve the truth, don't you, Ben? After all, it isn't that long ago that you told me that you loved me. I have to say that you have a very strange way of showing it!'

A rim of colour touched his pale cheeks. 'I know what I said. And I know what you didn't say. You made it perfectly plain at the time how you felt, Anna. All right, so you want the truth, do you? Well, the truth is that I don't want your pity!'

'Pity?' she repeated numbly, struggling to make sense of what he was saying.

'Yes!' His dark eyes glinted dangerously as he glared up at her. 'That's what this is all about, isn't it? You feel sorry for me because you think that I'm going to be crippled. Well, thank you very much but, no, thanks! I don't want your charity.'

She was so stunned that she didn't know what to say. Surely Ben didn't believe such rubbish?

It seemed so incredible that she didn't know whether to laugh or cry until she saw the anguish in his eyes. She was still struggling to find a way to convince him that he was completely wrong about her motives when he continued, and she went cold when she heard the finality in his voice.

'Anyhow, I've had time to think while I've been lying here. There isn't much else to do so it tends to concentrate your mind, you understand. I've realised that I made a mistake.'

'A mistake?' she repeated woodenly.

'Yes. I'm sorry, Anna, but I think I got rather carried away that night we spent together. I'm sure we are both adult enough to accept that these things happen from time to time, especially when life has been stressful.'

Like that day had been, she thought sickly. That had been the day Lucy Wilkins had tried to kill herself, and Ben had been very upset about what had gone on. But was he really trying to claim that the only reason he had made love to her was because it had been a sort of…of release from all the emotional pressure?

She didn't want to believe that, yet it was hard not to when he had sounded so certain. Hadn't she wondered if he'd started to have second thoughts after the accident? It all seemed to fit but she had to be absolutely sure.

'So what you're really saying is that you don't love me? Is that it, Ben?'

His lids lowered abruptly, almost as though he was too ashamed to look at her. 'That's right. I don't love you, Anna. I'm sorry but I'm sure you understand that it's better to be truthful.'

She bit her lip as she felt a wave of hysterical laughter bubbling inside her. She had gone to the hospital that night with the express intention of being truthful. How ironic that Ben had beaten her to it!

She left the ward without another word. What could she have said after that? Telling Ben that she loved him was out of the question now. Even if he believed her, he would only be embarrassed by the disclosure, and that was the last thing she wanted to do—embarrass him or herself. It was far better to say nothing than say something they would both regret.

Anna moved out of the flat over the surgery three days later. She had deliberately chosen the weekend because it meant that she didn't need to tell anyone where she was going. She simply wrote Adam a note, telling him that she had found somewhere else to live, and pushed it through the surgery door along with the keys.

She had paid three months' advance rental on a bedsit which the estate agency had found for her. The fact that the property had been vacant for some time was a good indication of the state of the place, but it would do. It was better than staying in Winton and being constantly reminded of what had happened.

The room was on the top floor of a dilapidated terraced house in one of the less salubrious areas of Manchester. Its main recommendation was that it came fully furnished, its biggest drawback the number of stairs that needed to be climbed to reach it. Anna knew that she wouldn't be able to stay there after the baby was born because hauling a pram up and down all the stairs would be a nightmare. It was simply a stopgap, like the job in Winton had been, although, hopefully, this venture wouldn't end so badly.

The days seemed to drag. She spent a lot of time in the nearby park because she hated sitting in the dingy room all day long. The weather was mild for the time of year and as long as she wrapped up warmly she enjoyed being outside. She didn't get in touch with anyone from the surgery and took care not to go anywhere she might bump into people she knew. That episode in her life was over. She had to look to the future now, although it was painful to think about a future that didn't feature Ben in it.

Christmas Day arrived, a day like any other, which she spent sitting in the park. There were a lot of people about—family groups walking off the effects of a heavy Christmas lunch and children trying out new bicycles and roller blades. Anna enjoyed watching them having fun, although it hurt to be reminded how alone in the world she was. She found herself wondering what Ben was doing and if he was still in hospital or at home in the cottage. Maybe he was spending the day with Adam and Beth, watching Hannah opening her presents. She sighed as she realised how quickly her thoughts had turned to him. Wherever he was, she doubted whether he was thinking about her.

She made her way back home through the growing dusk, wishing that she hadn't stayed out in the cold so long when she felt the nagging ache in the small of her back. She turned on both bars of the little electric fire as soon as she got in and made herself a cup of tea, but the pain wouldn't go away. Then, to cap it all, the electricity meter ran out and she didn't have any money to put in it.

Anna sighed as she considered her options. There would be no shops open on Christmas Day, which left her with the choice of sitting in the cold and dark or knocking on her neighbours' doors to see if they had any change. Although she hated to disturb them, she couldn't sit there all night, freezing to death.

She found her purse then went to see if there was anyone in. The room next to hers was empty, but she could hear the sound of a television coming from below. She made her way downstairs, gasping when a searing pain suddenly shot through her back. It was so strong that she had to stop and take a deep breath, and it had barely passed when another one hit her, this one seeming to envelop the whole of her lower body.

Anna clung hold of the bannister rail, feeling her heart racing as she realised that she was in labour. The baby wasn't due for more than three weeks but there was no doubt in her mind that that was what was happening.

She waited until the pain had eased sufficiently then made her way to the ground floor. There was a pay phone in the entrance hall so she used it to phone for an ambulance. The contractions were getting stronger now and she sent up a silent prayer that the baby wouldn't arrive before the ambulance got there. She couldn't bear the thought of the child being born there in the hall with no one around to help her. All of a sudden she found herself wishing that Ben was there with her, but there was no point wishing for something she couldn't have. Ben didn't love her, he never had. It had all been a dreadful mistake!

Two hours later Anna held her newborn son in her arms. She felt tears well in her eyes as she looked at his crumpled little face and realised how like Jo he looked. The midwife smiled as she came back to the bed to check on her.

'Worth all the pain and strain, was he?' she teased.

Anna summoned a sad little smile. 'You have no idea how much this baby means to me.'

'I've read your notes.' The midwife patted her hand kindly. 'This is your sister's child, isn't it? Do you want me to let her know what's happened? I'm surprised she didn't come in with you. Didn't you have chance to get a message to her?'

'My sister died,' she explained hollowly.

'Oh, I'm sorry! I had no idea.' The midwife sighed sadly. 'How awful for you in the circumstances. It's the kind of thing that you can't plan for, isn't it? Anyway, is there anyone else you'd like me to get in touch with, then? Another relative or a friend, perhaps?'

'No, there's no one.' Anna pressed a kiss to the baby's downy head. She took a deep breath but there was no way that she could avoid facing up to the truth. 'It's just the two of us from now on, but that's fine. We'll manage. We don't need anyone else.'

The midwife didn't say anything else, but Anna had a feeling that she didn't agree. Maybe the woman believed that everyone needed someone to help them, and maybe she was right.

She felt a piercing pain shoot through her heart and cuddled the baby closer, drawing comfort from the feel of his tiny body in her arms. The one person *she* needed wasn't interested in her or her child. There was no point pretending otherwise because she had to get used to the idea. Ben had his life to lead and she had hers. Their paths would never cross again in the future.

Anna was transferred to the maternity ward a short time later. It was the early hours of the morning by then so she was put in a side room rather than disturb the rest of the mums in the main ward. She had a cup of tea that one of the nurses made for her then fell fast asleep, worn out by everything that had happened. When she awoke it was the middle of the morning and there was someone sitting beside her bed. She felt her heart turn over when she saw who it was.

CHAPTER ELEVEN

'HELLO, Anna. How are you?'

'Wh-what do you want, Ben? Why are you here?'

Anna heard the shrillness in her voice and bit her lip when she saw that Ben had heard it too. She pushed herself up against the pillows, staring at him with troubled eyes. Her mind was racing this way and that but she couldn't work out why he had come to see her, let alone how he had known that she was in hospital.

'I've been looking for you for weeks,' he explained, and she shivered when she heard the grating note in his voice. He sounded as though he had been suffering an extreme kind of torment, yet she couldn't understand what was wrong.

'Why were you looking for me? I don't understand...'

'Because I've been going out of my mind, wondering what had happened to you! Dammit, Anna, didn't you realise how worried everyone would be when you upped and left like that? Did it never occur to you to tell anyone where you were going?'

She blinked when she heard the fury in his voice. She cast him an uncertain look, feeling her heart starting to race when she saw the hollows in his cheeks, the new lines around his eyes. Ben looked like a man who had been put through the emotional wringer, but why? Because he had been worried about her? She didn't want to let herself believe that but it was hard to dismiss the idea.

'I thought it best if I made a clean break,' she told him quietly, struggling to hold onto her composure.

'And that's why you disappeared off the face of the earth, is it?' His tone was harsh yet beneath the anger she could hear the pain that laced each word and her racing heart simply beat all the faster.

'What did you expect me to do?' she countered. 'You'd made it perfectly clear that you weren't interested what happened to me—'

'I lied.'

The terse admission stopped her dead. Anna stared at him, her grey eyes as big as saucers. 'You *lied*? What do you mean?'

'Exactly what I said,' he shot back. 'I lied when I told you that I didn't love you. I lied when I said that I'd only spent the night with you because of what had happened that day. I'm not proud of what I did, and I've paid a hundred times over for it, believe me, but I lied.'

All of a sudden the anger seemed to drain from him and she saw tears fill his eyes. Reaching over, he caught hold of her hand and lifted it to his lips. 'Oh, Anna, I love you so much. I've gone through hell these past weeks, wondering where you were and how you were managing. I know what I did was unforgivable but I had my reasons or, at least, I thought I had.'

'You love me?' she said numbly. She took a deep breath, wondering if she was hallucinating. This couldn't be happening. Ben couldn't be here sitting there, telling her that he loved her!

'Yes.' He kissed her fingers then looked deep into her shocked eyes. 'I love you with all my heart, Anna Clemence. I know I don't deserve a second chance but I'm hoping that you'll find it in your heart to forgive me. I want to spend my whole life taking care of you and our baby if you'll let me.'

'Our baby?' she said wonderingly.

'That's what he'll be if you allow me back into your life, darling. He'll belong to both of us, to you and me. I...I hope that you'll let me be a real father to him.'

His voice broke at that point and he couldn't go on. Anna felt a lump come to her throat when she saw the raw emotion on his face. There wasn't a doubt in her mind at that moment that Ben was telling her the truth, and it was impossible to hide how much it meant to her.

Tears streamed down her face and she heard him utter a rough little sound when he saw them. He pulled her towards him, cradling her in his arms, holding her as though he would never let her go again. 'Don't cry, my love. Please, don't cry. I can't bear to see you unhappy,' he whispered brokenly.

Anna gave a watery little laugh. 'I'm not unhappy. I just can't believe this is actually happening. It's like all my dreams have suddenly come true.' She took a deep breath then drew back so that she could look at him. 'I love you, too, Ben. I should have told you how I felt before now but I was afraid.'

'I know.' He smiled into her eyes when she looked at him in surprise. 'Beth told me what you had said to her in the hospital after the accident. I think she was trying to make me see what a mess I'd made of everything.'

'Is that why you decided to try and find me?' she asked gently, not really caring if it had been the reason. Ben was here and he loved her. Nothing else mattered except that!

'No. I'd already made up my mind that I was going to find you even if it took me the next hundred years to track you down,' he declared, looking at her in a way that made her heart drum. 'What Beth told me only proved to me what a fool I'd been!'

She laughed at that. 'I think we were both rather foolish. I should have told you sooner that I loved you...'

'I understand why you didn't, though.' He kissed her gently on the mouth. His eyes were tender as he looked at her. 'Beth told me what your brother-in-law said to you. It's no wonder that you were afraid of making a mistake.'

'I couldn't bear the thought that you might come to regret having fallen in love with me,' she admitted. She sighed when she saw the pain that crossed his face. 'I know now that I was wrong, Ben, but I didn't want to do anything that might end up hurting you or the baby.'

'So, rather than do that, you turned your back on everyone you knew and decided to go it alone?' he whispered huskily, and she could hear the anguish in his voice.

'It seemed the best thing to do,' she confessed. 'I never meant to worry everyone.'

Ben sighed heavily as he ran his hand down her cheek to wipe away the tears. 'We've all been worried about you, Anna. When Adam came to the hospital and told me that you'd moved out of the flat and that he had no idea where you'd gone, I think I went a little bit crazy. He had the devil of a job stopping me signing myself out there and then.'

'I'm glad he did.' She shuddered at the thought of him risking his health to find her.

He kissed her lightly on the mouth then drew back reluctantly. 'He only managed it because he promised that he would do everything he could to find out where you'd gone. Quite frankly, I've been at my wits' end these past weeks because he couldn't find a trace of you.'

'I didn't want to be found,' she admitted guiltily as she realised how much trouble she had caused. 'That's why I found a bedsit in the city. I knew that the chances of me bumping into anyone I knew in an area like that were very slim.'

'No wonder Adam couldn't find you.' Ben's expression

was grim. 'I dread to think how you've been managing these past weeks. It was pure good luck that I found out you'd been brought into the maternity unit last night otherwise I might never have discovered where you had gone to.'

Anna shivered at the thought. 'I'm so sorry. But how did you find out that I was here?'

'Eileen's daughter came in with a patient last night. You remember that she's a community midwife?' She nodded and he continued. 'She heard one of the staff mentioning your name and remembered Eileen telling her how worried everyone was because you'd disappeared. She phoned her mother and Eileen immediately phoned Adam and told him that you were here. It was all systems go after that.'

'Really?'

'Really.' He dropped a kiss on the tip of her nose and smiled at her. 'I kicked up such a fuss that Adam agreed to drive me here even though it was almost midnight. Unfortunately, I couldn't manage it under my own steam.' He tapped the arm of the chair and she gasped when she realised that it wasn't just one of the ordinary hospital chairs but a wheelchair.

Her heart twisted painfully as she gripped his hand. 'Are you using that because you can't walk? Tell me the truth, Ben. I need to know, not because it makes a scrap of difference to how I feel about you...'

'I know it doesn't,' he said softly, kissing her again. 'I know that you love me, Anna. And if that sounds smug, I have no intention of apologising for it!'

He smiled at her with a wealth of love in his eyes. 'I'm using the chair purely because it's easier for me to get around at the moment. I was extremely fortunate because my spine was only badly bruised. There's some residual stiffness but I'm having physio and that will sort it out eventually, although it's going to be a few months before I'm completely recovered.'

'Oh, I'm so glad!' she declared, smiling at him. 'I've been worried sick about you but I daren't phone Adam and Beth to find out how you were in case they somehow tracked me down.'

'You didn't want to be found, but you aren't sorry, are you, Anna?' He took a deep breath and his voice seemed to grate. 'Maybe I've sprung this on you too soon. I understand if you need time to think about it.'

'Think about what?' she asked, puzzled. 'About whether or not I love you?'

'That plus whether you can bear the thought of spending the rest of your life with me.' He kissed her palm, his lips warm and tender as he touched the soft flesh. 'I want you for ever and always, my love. But I don't want to talk you into doing something that doesn't feel right to you simply because I've caught you at a…well, at a weak moment.'

She laughed. 'So you're worried in case you might be taking advantage of me, are you, Dr Cole?' She slid her arms around his neck and drew him gently towards her. 'It sounds as though you need a little reassurance.'

'Not just a little,' he whispered against her lips. 'You might have to repeat the treatment at frequent intervals.'

'Sounds good to me,' she agreed, then stopped talking because there were more important things to think about. The kiss was everything they could have wished for except that it was far too short. They broke apart when an exaggeratedly noisy burst of coughing from the direction of the door alerted them to the fact that they had an audience.

'I hate to interrupt,' the young nurse told them, grinning, 'but you have one very hungry little boy in the nursery, demanding his breakfast. Shall I fetch him in?'

Anna smiled. 'Oh, yes, please.'

Ben laughed as the nurse went away. 'Think that was our first lesson about the joys of parenthood?'

'That baby comes first?' Her face suddenly sobered. 'You are sure that this is what you want, Ben? Having a baby is a big responsibility—'

'And an even bigger joy.' He stopped her with a kiss. 'This is what I want, Anna, and I don't have any doubts whatsoever. I'm probably in a better position than most people to understand all the pros and cons of being a step-parent.'

'What do you mean?' she asked uncertainly.

He sighed and his expression was sad all of a sudden. 'I told you that my mother was a single parent, didn't I? What I didn't tell you was that she had to bring me up on her own because the man she had been going out with told her that he didn't want anything to do with her when he found out that she was pregnant. It turned out that he was married and he had overlooked mentioning it before.'

'Oh, how awful for her!' she exclaimed, then gasped. 'That's why you were so shocked when you thought I might have been having an affair with a married man, wasn't it?' She sighed when he nodded. 'How sad for your mother and for you, too.'

'Mum didn't tell me the truth for a long time. She always refused to talk about my father whenever I asked her.' He sighed deeply. 'I think she was trying to stop me feeling rejected and also she found it difficult to talk about what had happened.'

'Because she was ashamed of the way she had been duped?' Anna guessed.

'Yes. It wasn't her fault but it took her a long time to understand that she had nothing to feel guilty about. I just wish that she had told me sooner rather than bottling it all up, though. I'm sure it would have been easier for both of

us to have everything out in the open rather than live with
the feeling that there was some sort of dark secret lurking
in the background.'

It explained so much about the way he had reacted to
her situation, Anna thought. No wonder he had been so
keen to ensure that she would tell her own child the truth
and not make the same mistake. 'Did she ever meet anyone
else?' she asked gently.

'Yes. I was about twelve when she met David. He was
a great guy, couldn't have been a more wonderful father to
me, in fact. He nursed Mum when she was taken ill a couple of years later, until she died, then looked after me and
put me through university.'

He paused and she could see the pain in his eyes. 'He
contracted Alzheimer's during my last year in med school.
I looked after him for as long as I could, which was why
I found it easier to do locum work. It meant that I could
take time off whenever I needed to and didn't have all the
extra responsibility that would have come with a permanent
post.'

'Didn't you have anyone to help you?'

'I had a succession of carers to look after him while I
was at work but they tended not to stay very long,' he
explained.

'It isn't easy, dealing with someone suffering from
Alzheimer's,' she observed quietly, knowing that it was a
massive understatement. She couldn't begin to imagine
how difficult it must have been for Ben over the years and
was filled with admiration for his devotion.

'It isn't. Seeing someone you love deteriorate is particularly painful,' he agreed sadly. 'David died last year, and
it was a blessing in a way, although I miss him dreadfully.'
He took a deep breath. 'However, recalling how he treated
me—how much he loved me—makes me certain that it

isn't a question of blood ties that create a bond between a child and a parent. I shall love this baby just as much as I would love my natural children.'

'I know you will,' she said, and realised that it was true. She took a deep breath as the nurse came back, carrying the baby, and felt her heart fill with joy. Ben would love this precious child as much as she would—as much as Jo would have done, in fact.

'He's quietened down a bit. Maybe he just wanted a cuddle,' the nurse told them. She looked expectantly from one to the other. 'So who wants first hold, then?'

Anna smiled at her. 'Let his daddy hold him first.'

'Thank you,' Ben whispered, and she could hear the ache in his voice. He cradled the little boy against his chest as the nurse gently laid the baby in his arms, and Anna knew that she had never seen anything that had looked so right, so perfect as Ben looked at that moment.

This precious baby had a father who would love and care for him for the rest of his life and she had a lifetime of love and happiness to look forward to. She felt truly blessed.

Three months later…

'Everything is arranged. The vicar is going to christen Daniel after morning service next Sunday.'

Ben came into the room, pausing automatically beside the crib where little Daniel was sleeping. Anna saw him smile as he gently drew the covers over the child. 'He's fast asleep now.'

'So he should be after keeping us awake all night,' Anna retorted. Her face filled with love as she looked at the baby. 'He's a real little monster.'

'Your mummy doesn't mean that, Daniel,' Ben said immediately, grinning at her. 'She loves you to bits, really.'

He looped his arms around her waist and pulled her to him, kissing her swiftly on the mouth. 'The same as I do.'

Anna sighed because there was no doubt in her mind that he was telling the truth. Day after day Ben had proved how much he loved the little boy and she could scarcely believe that she'd had so many doubts just a few short weeks ago.

She had moved into Lilac Cottage with the baby after she'd left hospital. She had been deeply touched to discover that Adam and Beth had decorated the nursery for her, taking it upon themselves to do the job as Ben had been unable to do it. There had been everything there that she could have wished for—a lace-trimmed crib, as well as a cot, clothes and toys and the more mundane nappies and toiletries. Beth had told her that Ben had asked her to buy whatever was needed and not worry about the cost.

Anna had wept when she had seen all the lovely things because she had known that she would never have been able to provide them for Daniel herself. However, it wasn't just the material support that meant so much to her but the fact that Ben was always there when she needed him. She knew that she had been incredibly lucky to find someone like him, and told him so.

'I'm the lucky one,' he said firmly. 'I never thought that I could be this happy, Anna.'

She rubbed her cheek against his, loving the feel of his arms around her. His back was healing slowly and as long as he didn't try to do too much, he could walk around without any difficulty and would be returning to work the following week.

'Me, too. Or is it neither?' she whispered.

'Who cares?' He kissed her slowly, lingeringly, smiling against her mouth when he felt the shiver that rippled through her. His tone was just the tiniest bit smug. 'Do you

really want to have an in-depth discussion about the se-
mantics of that statement?'

'It depends,' she said pertly.

He kissed her again, even more slowly and thoroughly
this time. 'On what?'

Anna smiled when she heard the thread of passion in his
voice that he couldn't quite disguise. 'On what else is on
offer. I mean, there's washing to do, and I haven't even
seen the vacuum cleaner for almost a week. Then there's
gardening and—'

'Enough!' he groaned. 'You're making me feel dizzy,
just thinking about all the work that needs doing in here.'
His smile was decidedly wicked now. 'In fact, I think I
need to have a lie down.'

'Really?' She raised her brows.

'Really,' he confirmed, kissing her again before steering
her towards the nursery door. 'Feel like joining me?'

'I don't feel sleepy, funnily enough,' she replied, feeling
her heart starting to race when she saw the expression in
his eyes. That Ben wanted her as much as she wanted him
wasn't in any doubt and their love-making had been everything she could have wished for.

'Neither do I,' he said, quickly pulling her into their bedroom and closing the door. He kissed her long and hard
then framed her face between his hands and looked at her.
'I love you, Anna Clemence, but there's just one thing that
keeps worrying me.'

She looked at him in surprise. 'What do you mean?'

'That it doesn't seem right that we should have two different surnames. That's not what a real family should have.
We should share the same name, wouldn't you agree?'

She felt her heart roll over when she realised what he
meant. 'Are you asking me to marry you, Ben?'

'I am, although it isn't the only thing I want to ask you.'

He dropped to one knee, catching hold of her hand and holding onto it as he smiled up at her. 'Will you do me the honour of becoming my wife?'

'Oh, yes!' She felt tears of joy come to her eyes and blinked them away, then frowned. 'But you said there was something else that you wanted to ask me?'

'That's right.' He took a deep breath as he stood up, as though he was unsure what her answer would be to his next question. 'I said that I wanted us to be a real family so will you let me adopt Daniel after we are married? That way he will be my son legally.'

The tears flowed down her cheeks because there was no way that she could contain her joy any longer. 'If it's what you really want—' she began.

'It is.' He pulled her back into his arms, holding her so close that she could feel the shudder of relief that ran through him when she whispered, 'Yes.'

'You don't know how happy you've made me, Anna,' he said brokenly, his voice catching. 'To know that I'll be your husband and Daniel's father makes me feel as though I'm the luckiest man alive.'

'We're the lucky ones,' she told him, standing on tiptoe so that she could kiss him, 'because we found you, Ben.'

He kissed her back, drawing her to him, holding her against his heart. 'I love you, Anna.'

'I love you, too,' she told him.

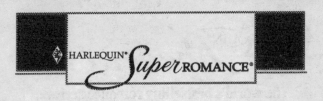

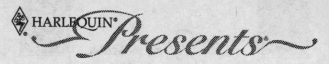

HARLEQUIN Presents

The world's bestselling romance series...
The series that brings you your favorite authors,
month after month:

Helen Bianchin...Emma Darcy
Lynne Graham...Penny Jordan
Miranda Lee...Sandra Marton
Anne Mather...Carole Mortimer
Susan Napier...Michelle Reid

and many more uniquely talented authors!

Wealthy, powerful, gorgeous men...
Women who have feelings just like your own...
The stories you love, set in exotic, glamorous locations...

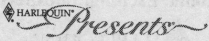

Seduction and passion guaranteed!

Harlequin® Historical

From rugged lawmen and valiant knights to defiant heiresses and spirited frontierswomen, Harlequin Historicals will capture your imagination with their dramatic scope, passion and adventure.

*Harlequin Historicals...
they're too good to miss!*

HARLEQUIN®

AMERICAN *Romance*

Invites *you* to experience the most upbeat, all-American romances around!

Every month, we bring you four strong, sexy men, and four women who know what they want—and go all out to get it.

We'll take you from the places you know to the places you've dreamed of.
Live the love of a lifetime!

AMERICAN *Romance*—
Heart, Home & Happiness

HARLEQUIN®
Makes any time special®

Visit us at www.eHarlequin.com

HARDIR1

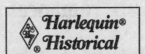